210,14

SKELETONS

IN THE CLOSET

As Elizabeth Linington:

SKELETONS IN THE CLOSET
CONSEQUENCE OF CRIME
NO VILLAIN NEED BE
PERCHANCE OF DEATH
CRIME BY CHANCE
PRACTISE TO DECEIVE
POLICEMAN'S LOT
SOMETHING WRONG
DATE WITH DEATH
NO EVIL ANGEL
GREENMASK!
THE PROUD MAN
THE LONG WATCH
MONSIEUR JANVIER
THE KINGBREAKER
ELIZABETH I (*Ency. Brit.*)

As Egan O'Neill:

THE ANGLOPHILE

As Lesley Egan:

MOTIVE IN SHADOW
THE HUNTERS AND THE
    HUNTED
LOOK BACK ON DEATH
A DREAM APART
THE BLIND SEARCH
SCENES OF CRIME
PAPER CHASE
MALICIOUS MISCHIEF
IN THE DEATH OF A MAN
THE WINE OF VIOLENCE
A SERIOUS INVESTIGATION
THE NAMELESS ONES
SOME AVENGER, ARISE
DETECTIVE'S DUE
MY NAME IS DEATH

RUN TO EVIL
AGAINST THE EVIDENCE
THE BORROWED ALIBI
A CASE FOR APPEAL

As Dell Shannon:

CASE PENDING
THE ACE OF SPADES
EXTRA KILL
KNAVE OF HEARTS
DEATH OF A BUSYBODY
DOUBLE BLUFF
ROOT OF ALL EVIL
MARK OF MURDER
THE DEATH-BRINGERS
DEATH BY INCHES
COFFIN CORNER
WITH A VENGEANCE
CHANCE TO KILL
RAIN WITH VIOLENCE
KILL WITH KINDNESS
SCHOOLED TO KILL
CRIME ON THEIR HANDS
UNEXPECTED DEATH
WHIM TO KILL
THE RINGER
MURDER WITH LOVE
WITH INTENT TO KILL
NO HOLIDAY FOR CRIME
SPRING OF VIOLENCE
CRIME FILE
DEUCES WILD
STREETS OF DEATH
APPEARANCES OF DEATH
COLD TRAIL
FELONY AT RANDOM
FELONY FILE
MURDER MOST STRANGE
THE MOTIVE ON RECORD

SKELETONS
IN THE CLOSET

ELIZABETH LININGTON

DOUBLEDAY & COMPANY, INC.

GARDEN CITY, NEW YORK

All of the characters in this book
are fictitious, and any resemblance
to actual persons, living or dead,
is purely coincidental.

This one is for my cousin
Lee Lennington, Jr.,
in the pious hope that his genealogical researches
will not turn up more black sheep in the
family records

Chaos of thought and passion, all confused;
Still by himself abused, or disabused;
Created half to rise, and half to fall;
Great lord of all things, yet a prey to all;
Sole judge of truth, in endless error hurled;
The glory, jest, and riddle of the world.
                              —Alexander Pope
                              An essay on man

Hurried and worried until we're buried, and
              there's no curtain call—
Life's a very funny proposition, after all.
                              —George M. Cohan

CHAPTER 1

It was sprinkling slightly as Maddox turned left on Cole from Fountain Avenue, and into the parking lot behind the Hollywood station. He was late; the ancient Maserati had been stubborn about starting. He was thinking halfway seriously about a new car; if Sue was starting a family they'd need another sedan, and her old Chrysler was on its last legs. By a couple of lucky chances the new-old house in Glendale was clear of payments, and it might make economic sense to buy something brand-new and let Sue drive the Maserati until it fell to pieces.

Everybody else was in; it was twenty to nine. This was the second rain they had had, and only the first week in November; evidently southern California was going to have another wet winter, after the usual baking-hot summer.

Maddox went in the back door of the station house, past the door to their modest laboratory, the rest rooms, to the big communal detective office across the hall from the small office relegated to Sue and Daisy. Sergeant Daisy Hoffman, slim and trim and blond, not resembling remotely the grandmother she was, looked up as he paused in the doorway.

"D-day," she said.

"Well, her appointment's for two o'clock. The doctor's supposed to have the results on the tests." It was Sue's day off.

"Fingers crossed," said Daisy seriously.

"I don't know," said Maddox. "It's a lunatic world to bring innocent children into." He turned across to the big office, shrugging off his trench coat.

The business of the day was already started. Rodriguez was talking to a citizen at his desk, taking notes; Feinman was on the phone. D'Arcy was brooding over a report. There was no sign of anybody else —probably already out on the legwork—and the door to Ellis's office across the hall was shut.

They had, as usual, this and that on hand: the perennial heists and burglaries to make the endless paperwork, the occasional corpses, the monotonous daily round of crime.

"And what delayed you?" asked D'Arcy.

"Car wouldn't start. I'm thinking about a new one."

"Who can afford the payments? Those heisters hit again." D'Arcy handed over the report: the night-watch report. "The same pair, by the descriptions."

"Hell," said Maddox mildly.

"Two other heists, entirely anonymous, and four more burglaries," said D'Arcy morosely. "All the damn paperwork, and nowhere to go on any of it. Naturally."

"What we're paid to do," said Maddox. "Busywork." He opened his notebook and lit a cigarette. The immediate busywork on his agenda was getting a statement from that pharmacist who'd been held up on Monday night; he was supposed to come in at nine-thirty.

"Nolan and Dowling went out on this liquor-store heist." D'Arcy sniffed. "Let's hope they remember all the standard questions."

"Now, D'Arcy," said Maddox inattentively. The phone rang on D'Arcy's desk.

"Well, after what Bill pulled on that homicide, forgetting to search the body—when I think of anybody making rank at twenty-six, for God's sake—" D'Arcy reached a hand to the phone.

"Give him time." There had been a few changes at the Hollywood station, L.A.P.D., in the last couple of months. Lieutenant Roseman, who had been coasting along anticipating retirement and doing as little as possible, had finally retired in August, and George Ellis had been promoted to lieutenant and his office. They had gotten three new detectives to add to the strength. Roger Stacey was an experienced man from the Hollenbeck station and had gone to beef up the night watch; Lee Dowling and Bill Nolan had just graduated from uniform to plainclothes, but experience would make them more useful in time.

"D'Arcy . . . So what've we got now? Oh. Oh, well, that's got to be— Yeah. What's the location? O.K., we're on it." D'Arcy put down the phone. "More new business. And it's got to be that kid."

"What kid?"

"In Donaldson's report. Reported missing last night—it didn't get sent up here until after midnight, naturally the Traffic men didn't think it was any big deal, but by what Ken left us, the father finally convinced them the kid wasn't a runaway type and they did a little looking around. Now we've got a body, and ten to one it's him. That was the desk—Traffic just called in. Kid's body in an alley out on Sunset."

Maddox abandoned his notebook and glanced over the night-watch report. There wasn't much on it: Roy Kelsey, reporting his thirteen-year-old son missing—Robert Kelsey, a vague description, nondescript clothes, supposed to be home by dark.

"We'll have to go look at it anyway," said D'Arcy. Maddox sighed, got up and went over to Rodriguez' desk.

"If this pharmacist shows, ask him to wait or talk to him yourself, César. We seem to have a new homicide."

"Surprise, surprise," said Rodriguez.

It was raining a little harder. They took D'Arcy's old Dodge. The location was just down from the intersection of Sunset and Western, a narrow alley behind the shop fronts on Sunset; the squad car was parked at the mouth of the alley, behind a big trash-collection truck, and Patrolman Day was standing there with another man waiting for them.

"My God," the other man was exclaiming, probably for the dozenth time, as Maddox and D'Arcy came up, "I was late—I usually hit along here half an hour earlier, but there was a big mess at one place on Vermont, but anyways when I pulled in here, my God, I thought it was just a pile of old clothes and then when I looked, my God—and I didn't have a dime for the phone, I hadda get change at the drugstore on the corner—my God, it's just a kid—maybe a hit-run, but what a goddamn thing, just a kid—"

They looked. "Well, it's got to be the Kelsey kid," said D'Arcy, "doesn't it?"

"I think," said Maddox, "we'd better have some pictures." They didn't exchange any comments in front of the civilian, but at first glance they didn't think this was a hit-run. The boy was about average size for thirteen or so, lying facedown on the dirty blacktop of the alley, alongside a big dumpster crammed with trash. He was wearing jeans and a plaid shirt, and the jeans had been pulled halfway down his legs; on top of the upper half of the body was a blue quilted nylon jacket with a hood. He had curly blond hair, and just behind the left ear was a little mess of coagulated blood matting the curls.

"Yeah," said D'Arcy, and walked back to the squad to call the lab.

Maddox told the driver to get back on his route and collect the trash later. They'd be busy. Eventually the mobile lab truck showed up with Baker in it; he took some flash shots from various angles and a while after that the morgue wagon came. There wouldn't be much use poking around for possible scientific evidence at the scene. The doctors would pin down the time closer, but the body had probably been here all night. It had rained hard, briefly, in the early hours of the morning, and the boy's clothes were still sodden. The chances were that he had died somewhere else and been dumped here.

They drove back to the station and Maddox called the father. It was a modest address on Loma Linda. The night watch had just taken the bare information; there'd be details to get, but first of all they wanted a positive identification. It was one of the dirty jobs detectives came in for, breaking the bad news and escorting the relatives to identify bodies.

Roy Kelsey came into the office twenty minutes later. He was a big stocky man about thirty-five, with thinning fair hair and steady blue eyes in a round face. He wore a rumpled tan jump suit; he looked tired and his eyes were bloodshot. He said in a heavy voice, "Sergeant Maddox?—you're the one called—the desk sergeant said just to come back here. You've found Bobby—you said—"

"We don't know, Mr. Kelsey. We want you to look at a body," said Maddox gently. "We think it may be your son."

Kelsey sat down suddenly in the chair beside Maddox's desk. "A body," he said numbly. He looked at them, and around the big office, with a vague expression: at thin dark nondescript Maddox, long lanky D'Arcy looming over him—Rodriguez slouching at his desk talking on the phone, Feinman hunched over his typewriter pecking at a report, Rowan talking to a raddled-looking blond woman and taking notes. The rain was streaming thinly down the tall windows. "A body," said Kelsey.

"We're very sorry, sir. But if you can tell us definitely—"

"Yeah," said Kelsey. "Yeah, sure. Whatever I got to do—O.K."

At first, sitting in the front seat of the Dodge, he was silent. Then he began to talk. He said, "Was it an accident? Somebody hit him? He's always careful in traffic—Bobby's an awful sensible kid, you know. Responsible. I told him, be home before dark, and he would have been— he always is. I can always trust Bobby—never had any worry about him. See, there's just the two of us now—my wife—Bobby's mother— died of cancer last year. She was only thirty-four. It was so sudden— just thought she was run-down, and then the doctor said— She was gone in three months. So there's just Bobby and me. I'm not at home when he gets back from school, I work at Nick's garage on Hillhurst, but I never worry about Bobby. I can trust him, you know? He said— yesterday morning—he was going out collecting for his paper route, after school. He delivers the *Herald*, see. And I said to him, you be home before dark, and he said sure, he would be. I got home as usual about six-twenty, and it was dark then. And when he wasn't home by seven, I knew—something must've happened. I called—and that first cop—asking if he'd ever run away before, if he was into drugs— Bobby! It made me mad—I tried to tell him that was just crazy—I knew something bad must've happened—"

At the morgue he stood over the tray and looked at the boy's face. The body had just been covered with a sheet: the doctors, the lab, would want to go over the clothes. The face was unmarked, curiously peaceful and very young-looking, a round freckled face with a snub nose.

"That's Bobby," said Kelsey dully. "Was it an accident?"

"We don't know yet, Mr. Kelsey."

"It wouldn't have been his fault. He was always careful in traffic. He was just down on Ardmore, Hobart, he only had the boulevard to cross, coming home. Maybe some drunk—" He turned away blindly. "We never went to church much. I don't know—about a funeral, a minister—"

"We'll let you know, sir," said Maddox. "You understand, there'll have to be an autopsy. We'd like to know what happened to him."

"Yeah," said Kelsey. "All right. But an accident—wouldn't have been his fault. He was always careful. He was a sensible kid."

Maddox and D'Arcy didn't tell him they doubted if it had been an accident. They drove him back to the station. The pharmacist had come in, said Rodriguez, and made a statement, but there wasn't anything in it, not a passable description of Monday night's heister. "But the pair who hit that bowling alley last night sound like this pair we've heard about before. I don't know what the hell Nolan and Dowling are doing on it, they're not back yet, but—"

Kelsey had gone. D'Arcy started to type a report, grumbling about paperwork, and Maddox called the morgue, got handed around a little before talking to one of the doctors. Bergner wasn't there; the doctor was one of the newest in the coroner's office, annoyed at the cops trying to tell him his job.

"Simmer down," said Maddox. "Of course you'll have a thorough look. I just thought you'd appreciate a shortcut, Doctor. As an educated guess, the boy was picked up by a pervert. We'd like to know yes or no as soon as possible."

"Not that there's much you can do about it if he was. They're a dime a dozen anywhere around—but they don't usually end up killing 'em, at that. Somebody'll be on it. We'll get back to you."

Maddox put the phone down and leaned back. He realized with

surprise that he was hungry. Somehow it had gotten to be after twelve, half the day gone and not much done. D'Arcy finished the initial report and they went out to lunch together, at a coffee shop on Fountain. They didn't discuss the Kelsey boy; it was a depressing and discouraging thing, and of course they didn't have any facts on it yet.

When they got back to the station, there was a man talking to Sergeant Whitwell at the front desk, a man dressed in black with a clergyman's back-to-front white collar. "Oh, God," said D'Arcy, "not another one."

"These are the detectives, sir, you can tell them about it," said Whitwell. "Mr. Honeycutt, Sergeant."

The clergyman was tall and spare, with a thin ascetic face and a surprising bass voice. "It is," he said, "an outrage. An outrage. The wanton destruction bad enough, but the implications—I was nearly sick when I saw—"

Maddox felt tired. Thank God, he thought, tomorrow was his day off. Just about now Sue would be in the doctor's office, getting the good news or the bad. He and D'Arcy took the Reverend Mr. Honeycutt into the detective office and heard what he had to say. There wasn't much they could do about it, but they had to go through the motions; the lab men would go over and take pictures for the records, dust the place for possible prints, and that would be the end of it.

Mr. Honeycutt's church was the seventh to be vandalized in the last five weeks. The builders of churches did not think first and foremost of burglar-proofing, and the vandals had gotten into the churches without much trouble, through basement windows and rear doors. There were no signs of the slick pro burglars, and of course no pro burglar would pick a church to hit; by all the evidence, the simple motive was the vandalism, and that said almost for sure that the vandals were juveniles, and even if they had left any prints they wouldn't be in records.

The only slight difference this time was that the vandalism had been even more wholesale, because Mr. Honeycutt's church had contained more to vandalize. All the other six churches had belonged to evangelical sects, which did not go in for the cushioned pews, elaborate communion services or religious statues; but Mr. Honeycutt was the spiritual leader of St. James' Episcopal Church on Hollywood Boulevard, one of the oldest in town and one of the most ornate. Subsequently, surveying the damage while the lab men started to poke around, Maddox felt a little cold anger at the mindlessness of it: the slashed cushions, knife gouges on the carved pews, hymn books ripped apart, the Bible from the lectern torn to pieces, the painted plaster statues broken to bits in the aisles. There were the usual obscenities scrawled on the walls, and one feature that had appeared only once before, in the latest case of a small Catholic church a few blocks away from here: besides the four-letter words in black spray paint were some others—ONLY FOUL BELIEVE GOD and GOD IS SATIN.

"Can one believe, Satanists?" exclaimed Mr. Honeycutt incredulously. "But of all the vile—I could hardly believe it when I—"

"No," said Maddox sadly. "I think mostly the ones who go in for black magic are better educated than to make elementary spelling mistakes. When had you been in the church last?"

"Not since Sunday night—the evening service. We have a Wednesday night candlelight service, and I had just come by to post the hymn numbers and leave my robes—I had, er, just picked up one set at the cleaners'—"

"What about your cleaning service, in the church I mean?"

"The janitorial crew comes in on Thursdays—my dear heaven, how they will ever clean up all this—I called Mr. Wilson, my curate, and the organist—we'll have to put off tonight's service, but dear heaven, all this terrible mess—"

"Yes, it *is* a mess," said Maddox. "And I'm afraid there's not much chance of laying hands on the vandals, Mr. Honeycutt." He went on to explain why, and Honeycutt exhibited some righteous anger.

The lab work was a waste of time, but just on the chance, it had to be done. Maddox was feeling even more tired. It had been an unproductive week so far, full of the tedious legwork and even more tedious paperwork. There was an unidentified corpse, picked up last Sunday night, of all places on the front lawn of the Hollywood Cemetery; it was the corpse of a man about twenty-five, and it had got to be a corpse by an O.D. of heroin, but that was all they knew about it. There were currently nine unsolved heists being worked, not including the three that had probably been pulled by the same pair: they had some good descriptions of those two, but it hadn't led anywhere yet, and one of those counts added up to attempted homicide, when they'd taken a shot at one victim who had showed a little resistance. The slug had been smashed on a cement wall, so the lab couldn't identify the gun, which wouldn't have been much help anyway. The perennial rash of burglaries had hit a new high last month, and there was never much to do about the burglaries either, except to hope that one of the burglars would leave a print already in records, and they could get the description of the loot on the hot list to all pawnbrokers. Since the Metro Squad had turned out last May to crack down on the hordes of prostitutes, of both sexes, infesting the main drags of town, that situation was a little better, but they were beginning to come out in daylight again and annoy the respectable citizens. It was about time—school had been open for a couple of months—that they had some gang rumbles on the campuses. And the narco business was always with them: the pushers recruiting new customers, the users out shoplifting and mugging for the wherewithal to get the supply. If there had ever been any glamor to the big town that was Hollywood, it was long gone and dead.

It was after three-thirty when they got back to the station, and he was anticipating the end of shift and getting home. There were times, and this was one of them, when he wondered why in God's name he had ever picked this thankless dirty job. But, small favors: at least he wasn't in the lab. The lab men would spend the rest of their shift at that church, and longer tomorrow, and turn up nothing useful for all the work.

At least the Maserati was running smoothly again—for how long was anybody's guess. He stopped at the rest room down the hall and, coming out, fished for change for the coffee machine, had just sorted out a quarter when Rodriguez came out of the office on his way to the back door. "So you can come along and look at a new homicide."

"Oh, don't tell me."

"The squad just called it in, I don't know what it is." Rodriguez, with his hairline mustache and sleek good looks, was usually a dapper dresser, but in this kind of weather his tailored Dacron suit was submerged in an ancient trench coat and he was wearing an unaccustomed slouch hat. It was raining harder, and turning cold. "It's down on Ardmore somewhere."

"So you can drive." Maddox went to get his coat, followed him out to the lot. "What a day. I'll be glad to get home."

"Going to be an early year, this much rain in November. And damn it, I've got a date tonight, I'll be damned if I stay overtime to write another report." Rodriguez shoved the Ford into reverse and backed out of the slot too fast.

"And when are you going to get decently married so you can stay home nights?" asked Maddox.

Rodriguez grinned. "I haven't come across one yet worth giving up all the others for, *amigo*. This one's a real honey—worth splurging on some. Taking her out to that French place in Beverly Hills."

"Ouch. That'll set you back."

Rodriguez was fiddling with the windshield wipers, which were reluctant to work. He got them going finally by the time he turned onto

Fountain. Twenty blocks through slow traffic, he turned down Ard-more. "It should be the next block or so, by the address." And a block farther on they spotted the squad car.

This was a tired section of old central Hollywood, all residential along these narrow old streets in between the main drags, Hollywood and Sunset boulevards, Fountain, Santa Monica Boulevard. A long time ago most of these streets had been lined with modest single houses on standard fifty-by-a-hundred-and-fifty lots; only occasionally would one of them have the rental unit in the backyard, or built on top of the garage. But in the last twenty-five years, with all of Los Angeles bulging at the seams and spreading out farther on every side, housing had been at a premium, and in a good many other areas besides this the single houses had been disappearing, giving way to large and small apartment houses, in the more affluent areas the condominiums. Along most of these streets there were just a few single houses left; ten years from now there wouldn't be any.

The squad was sitting at the curb in front of what had been one of those. Patrolman Cassidy was talking to three men on the sidewalk. There was a bulldozer just up from there; behind the bulldozer, in the middle of the city-sized lot, were the remains of a house.

"You've got one for the books here, Sergeant," said Cassidy.

"Just as we was about to knock off," said the biggest man of the three. He looked disgusted. "Oh, Jesus. My God. I mean, one bad enough, but two—"

"This is Mr. Tolliver. Sergeant Maddox, Detective Rodriguez."

"My God," said Tolliver. He was a big hairy fellow in his forties, bundled up in an old raincoat, shoulders hunched against the drizzle. "I hate rain. We got work ahead for six months, and the rain stops everything dead. And I knocked down a lot of houses but I never found a body under one before. Let alone two."

"Under the house?" Rodriguez was fascinated; he always liked the offbeat ones.

"Yeah. See, we're going to put up an apartment here. It wouldn't take much to knock the place down, one of these old frame houses been here maybe like sixty years—not but what a lot of those places were damn well built, hardwood floors and all. Me saving time." He spat disgustedly. "We been on another job down in Hawthorne, just after lunch it starts to rain, I say O.K., it's probably not raining further uptown, we get this job done instead. The 'dozer was already sitting here, I'd figured to do it tomorrow. So like you see we get it down mostly, but all these old places had pretty deep foundations, not like we

build now, and I'm just makin' a pass at one side when Tony yells at
me—"

"So let's have a look."

"It's your job to look at it," said Tolliver. "I'd just like to get out of
this damn rain and go home."

"Well, hang around awhile, we may have a couple of questions."
Maddox and Rodriguez followed Cassidy past the bulldozer. There was
a cement strip which had been the front walk leading up to the house.
At the right side of the lot they could see the remnants of what had
been twin cement strips constituting a driveway; at the rear of the lot a
single garage was still standing, a ramshackle frame building with a single door hanging rather drunkenly half open.

It was impossible to say what the original house had looked like; it
was just a heaped mass of old lumber strewn in piles. But the foundation was still visible, a little wall of cement in a vaguely rectangular pattern. The 'dozer had smashed in just one section of it, on the side away
from the driveway, and then backed off. "There you are," said Cassidy,
"and I wish the doctors luck on it."

"I'll be damned," said Maddox. And after a moment he added,
"You'd better go call up a morgue wagon. I don't know just what a
doctor could say, but this rain isn't helping to preserve any evidence."

"If there's any evidence left," said Rodriguez. He squatted to look
closer.

There was a jumbled mass of broken lumber nearby where the 'dozer
had knocked down walls, and just this side of that the broken cement
where a section of foundation had been caved in, leaving a little trench
a couple of feet deep. And rudely uplifted and uncovered by the 'dozer,
there were two bodies nearly side by side.

Visibly they were human bodies, but that was about all it was possible to say. Neither, as far as Maddox could see, was reduced to a skeleton; they looked partly mummified. Both had a few shreds of un-
identifiable clothing clinging to them. It wasn't possible to guess
whether they'd been male or female, or how long they might have been
here.

"It'll be interesting to hear what the doctors say," said Rodriguez.
"But I don't suppose the bodies buried under a house died peacefully
in bed. I will be damned."

"Yes, well, pending what the doctors say we'd better ask a few questions." Maddox straightened and went back down the walk to Tolliver.
"Who owns this property?"

"Keene and Adams Realty," said Tolliver. "I got no idea how long they've owned it, probably not too long. Or the house'd have got knocked down before now. Like a lot of other companies—realty people, private speculators—they've bought a few old places like this, tear down what's there and put up apartments. We've done four-five jobs for them."

The realty company could tell them who had owned the house. But who had owned it when the bodies were stashed under it? Together, or separately? And no doctor was going to be able to pin down a month or a year on those bodies. "Well, thanks." And it probably wouldn't be any use to set the lab men sifting through the dirt here, or would it?

"We can go? Well, thank God. What a hell of a thing." The crew departed thankfully. There wasn't anyone else around; the old frame house had been sandwiched between two medium-sized apartment buildings, and in this area most of the residents would be working people, away all day; in any case, the rain would keep people in.

"Hey, Ivor—come up here a minute." Rodriguez was beckoning. "Look, I think we can trace it down a little. Educated guess, they could have been under a closet floor."

"How do you make that out?" He joined Rodriguez and Cassidy inside the rectangle.

Rodriguez pointed. "Bathroom," he said succinctly. Mutely evident of the comforts of home, left in ruins by the 'dozer but still half attached to a length of pipe, there roughly at the middle rear of the rectangle was a broken toilet, parts of a washbasin beside it, more pipes. "You know how most of these old places from the twenties were laid out—how many of us grew up in one?"

"Not me. We had a Spanish stucco in Inglewood." And irrelevantly he had a sudden sharp memory of it—home—until the plane crash, his last year in high school. And no real home since—until Sue, and Margaret. "What about it?"

"Nine out of ten of them, the combination living-dining room across the front, with a front porch the same length. Kitchen and service porch one side, bedrooms and bathroom on the other." Rodriguez picked his way over the piled lumber. "About here there'd have been a hall leading off the front room, and probably a cross hall from the kitchen meeting it. The bathroom at the end of the first hall, here, and the kitchen was at the other side, there's the sink and pipes—two bedrooms along this side. And building was cheap back then, there'd have been good-sized walk-in closets."

"Right about here," said Cassidy. "Over where the bodies are."

"You're using some imagination," said Maddox.

"Not much," said Cassidy dryly. "My grandparents live in a place sort of like this, over in El Monte." He reached down and picked up something from the rubble. Miraculously whole, it was a wooden coat hanger.

"You'll make rank yet," said Maddox. The morgue wagon pulled up behind Rodriguez' Ford, and the attendants came up with a gurney.

They took a look, and one of them said, "My God, what you boys do come up with. No waiting on the scientific team?"

"Just what good do you think they could do?" asked Maddox reasonably. "Take them in, but handle with care in case there should be anything to interest the lab."

There wasn't anything more for them to do here, and while the rain had lessened to a thin sprinkle, it was turning much colder. There was that definite sharp tang in the air that said there had been snow in the back mountains; it was going to be an early winter, all right.

It was five-forty. Just time to start some follow-up before the end of shift. Rodriguez could write the initial report in the morning. They went back to the office and Maddox looked in the phone book; Keene and Adams Realty was listed on Sunset Boulevard. He was passed around through a couple of secretaries, finally talked to a fellow named Forslund, who was annoyed and uncooperative at first, turned helpful and enthralled when he heard what it was about.

"You're *police? Bodies?* Under a *house?* One of *our*—well, I will be good and goddamned. I will be—"

"We'd like to know when your firm bought the property and who owned it before." Maddox told him the address. "I suppose it'll be in your records."

"Oh, yes, certainly, Sergeant. I don't know anything about it myself, I've been on that shopping complex in La Habra, but there'll be records, of course. Hell and damnation," said Forslund, "I'd stay and look it up for you, Sergeant, but the staff's all left and it's my wife's birthday, I'm taking her out to dinner and the theater—"

"Tomorrow'll do," said Maddox. "Just so we get the information eventually."

"I'll get on it, or somebody, first thing. My God, Mr. Keene will have a fit—we'll get back to you first thing, Sergeant."

"Ask for Detective Rodriguez or D'Arcy. Tomorrow's my day off."

"Oh," said Forslund. He sounded a little surprised. "Well, O.K." Maddox put the phone down and thought amusedly, gentleman surprised I can just walk away from the big exciting mystery; news for him, it's just a job. A thankless job.

He yawned and got up. Everybody else had left. He hadn't seen George Ellis today at all—somebody had said something about him being at the D.A.'s office downtown. And he never had heard if Nolan and Dowling had come up with anything on the latest heist. The heists —he had had one little idea about that pair who had taken a shot at the proprietor of the music store—if he ever had ten minutes he wanted to knock that around with Ellis and Rodriguez. A music store. Funny place for heisters to hit.

He got out his keys on the way down the hall. He wondered if they'd ever get that body identified. And just what the doctors could say about the bodies under the house.

It had stopped raining altogether. The Maserati started obediently, and for a wonder traffic on the Glendale freeway was moving right along. He got off at Verdugo Road and went on up into Verdugo Woodlands. It was farther to drive, but the spacious old two-story house and big lot were worth it, and thank God, by the lucky circumstances, clear of any mortgage. It was at the end of a dead-end street, Starview Terrace. He pulled into the drive; Sue's Chrysler and Margaret's old Ford occupied the garage. As he came up to the back door it was flung open, and a single *basso profundo* comment indicated that Tama the Akita—the Japanese bear dog—acknowledged his arrival.

Sue flung her arms around him exuberantly. "Darling Ivor, we did it! It's official, and the baby's due about the middle of July—and I'm just fine—the doctor just said some extra vitamins—"

Maddox hugged her hard. "We did it. That's just fine, Sue. Darling Sue." He couldn't say all he felt; but she knew.

"It'll all work out just fine—I can go on working for six months and then take six months' leave without losing any seniority—I wish I could just quit and stay home, but we couldn't make it—and if you have to get a new car—and Mother's here to take over—and listen, Ivor, we've been arguing about names and I want—"

"Yes, yes," said Maddox.

"And I can't say," said Margaret Carstairs, "that I'm really looking forward to diapers and that messy baby food again, but it'll work out just fine." She twinkled at them, bent to open the oven door. "And we've got time for a drink before dinner. Celebrate the occasion."

Maddox grinned back at her. "Occasion to celebrate all right." In about twenty years, Sue was going to look a lot like Margaret, slim and dark and neatly good-looking, which was just fine with him.

"And I haven't had a bit of morning sickness yet—"

"Don't speak too soon," said Margaret amusedly. "You're only about three weeks along."

"Well, about names—" said Sue. "I've been thinking—I suppose half a glass of sherry wouldn't do me any harm—and I don't really care if it's a boy or a girl—but about names, Ivor—"

CHAPTER 2

And of course, thought Sue crossly as she drove the freeway to work on Thursday morning, her mother would always side with Ivor. The three-cornered argument they'd gotten into—

"Of course the very first thought I had about a girl was Margaret—"

"And I'll veto that right off. Not two in the same family, she'd be bound to pick up some obnoxious nickname—"

"Mmh, yes, I'll vote against that too," he'd said promptly. "The one and only Margaret is all we want."

"Well, all right"—nobody could say she wasn't reasonable—"we could use it as a middle name. Ann Margaret. Amanda Margaret. Jennifer Margaret."

"And you know that'd end up as Jenny, and I don't like that," he said definitely.

"Well. I did think of Jonathan for a boy. Or Hugh—or possibly Gerald—"

"Whoa. No. Going through life with an oddball name myself, I wouldn't wish anything remotely fancy on a boy. If it's a boy, it'll be John. Well, I'd have no objection to John Ivor—who uses a middle name much? But that's my final word."

"Oh, darling, it's so *ordinary!*"

But he wouldn't be moved—men—and of course her mother backed him up. Driving down the Glendale freeway, Sue thought that after all there was plenty of time, maybe she could argue him around some way.

It was a brilliant sparkling day of bright sunlight, and very cold and clear enough for a glimpse of the glistening snow on the back mountains. At the station she met Rodriguez just arriving and told him the news. D'Arcy was at the coffee machine at the rear of the hall, and she told him. In the office across from the big detective bureau she hugged Daisy, telling her. Daisy hugged her back and said warmly, "Congratulations. They're a lot of trouble and work and worry, but worth it. Of course you've been thinking about names—"

George Ellis looked in while they were talking about names, heard

the news and congratulated Sue absently. "A couple of witnesses to
those latest heists are due in to make statements, you can talk to
them."

They had fair descriptions of a couple of the recent heisters, but that
wasn't much use. On that pair three witnesses had given better descriptions, but hadn't made any mug shots. The first witness they listened to,
a liquor-store owner who'd been held up last night, didn't give them
anything useful: he couldn't say whether the man had been dark or
blond, big or medium, all he told them was that it was a big gun and
by the register tab he'd gotten away with nearly two hundred dollars.

But in the middle of the morning Mrs. Adeline Truax came in. She
was the fourth witness to describe the pair of heisters, and she was
more definite than the other three. She was a plump woman in her forties with a blunt plain face and rather improbable golden hair, and
eminently commonsensible. She and her husband owned the bowling
alley that had been held up on Tuesday night, and she had been alone
there when the heisters came in.

"I'm never there at night, Ed doesn't like it, not that we get any
rowdy customers—a lot of young people, but decent types. But he's
been in bed with the flu since Monday. Temperature of a hundred and
two that night, and of course the middle of the week's usually slow.
There was only one couple in, looked like high school kids, when these
louts showed up. They both had guns—oh, Lord, I couldn't say what
kind, but they looked pretty big—revolvers—I don't know much about
guns. But I'd know those guys again, especially the one I saw closest.
They were both big, six-one, six-two, and—you know—broad. Big.
The biggest one, the one who took the money, he was blonder than the
other one—they were maybe twenty-five, somewhere around there. His
ears stuck out, and he didn't have much forehead, his hair grew kind of
low down. I guess they both had on dark pants, but that one had on a
real loud yellow shirt—I'd sure know him if I saw him again—he had
a kind of square face, and a big mouth only his lips were thin— Well,
it had been a slow day, they only got about thirty dollars."

She was a better witness than the other three. The others hadn't
made any mug shots, but every avenue had to be explored. "Would you
have the time to look at some pictures?" asked Sue. "In our records?"

"Mug shots," said Mrs. Truax interestedly. "Be glad to. These louts
robbing people right and left, I'd like to help you catch up to 'em."

Sue drove her down to the R. and I. office at central headquarters and set her looking through the fat books of photographs on the chance that she could spot one.

The only way to work the heists, when there wasn't any physical evidence available, was to chase down the possible suspects with the suggestive records and lean on them; once in a while one came apart and admitted guilt. Everybody else was out doing that on Thursday morning at eleven o'clock, and Rodriguez and Feinman had just listened to an alibi from one of those and let him go, when a teletype came in from the Feds. The unidentified corpse dead of an O.D. wasn't in their records, so they had sent his prints to the FBI, and now the Feds identified him. He was Private Arthur Livesey, AWOL from the air force base at Vandenberg, which was up near San Luis Obispo. He had gone over the hill about two months ago.

"Loose ends," said Feinman resignedly. He got on the phone to Vandenberg Air Force Base and eventually talked to Livesey's immediate sergeant. Livesey had been a known dope user, had a dismal record with the Air Force; he was twenty-one, had been in the service less than a year. Good riddance, said the sergeant shortly, hearing he was dead. The damn-fool kids using the foolish powder. He could give them the name of Livesey's next of kin, a Mrs. Alice Livesey, an address in Houston. Feinman thanked him, called police headquarters in Houston and talked to a desk sergeant there. The Houston boys could break the news and ask about disposition of the body; if possible L.A. would like to save the cost of a funeral.

He was still talking to Houston when the desk relayed a call to Rodriguez. "Sergeant Maddox said to talk to you. This is Forslund, from Keene and Adams. Listen, I'm sorry as hell it took so long, but it was Bob Barlow handled the deal and he's out of town—I couldn't get hold of Mr. Keene right away, he was out looking at that property on Fairfax—but I've got the information for you now, on that house on Ardmore. I can't get over that damn thing—bodies under the house, for God's sake—"

"So, how long has the company owned it?" asked Rodriguez.

"It just got through a short escrow about a couple of weeks ago. We bought it from a Mrs. Joan Ogden in September. Her address is Pueblo Drive in Monterey Park. We paid ninety-five thousand for it, of course that was just the land value."

"Yes. Thanks so much," said Rodriguez. Forslund would have asked eager questions about the bodies, but he cut him off. He passed that on to Feinman, lit a new cigarette and told Whitwell to get him the coroner's office. After a delay he got Dr. Bergner. "We were just wondering if anybody's had a look at those bodies, Doctor. The bodies buried under the house."

"Well, I've had a look, that's all. Anything to be gotten won't be a hell of a lot, or soon—what do you expect? Not a hell of a lot there. I doubt if we can tell you how either of them died, but I haven't had a close look yet."

"All I'm after right now," said Rodriguez, "is a rough estimate of how old they are."

Bergner grunted. Rodriguez could visualize him rolling the inevitable cigar in his fat fingers. "Um. Not much less than two years—I think one of them is older than the other. Pending a close look, say four years at the outside."

"*Bueno*. And anything else you can eventually tell us—"

"I'll get to them presently. Or somebody will."

Rodriguez relayed that, and Feinman passed a ruminative hand across his long lantern jaw. "That's one of the funniest things we've had in a while. . . . Stop for lunch on the way to see this woman?—it's nearly noon."

"Let's see if the lady's at home first." Mrs. Joan Ogden was at home. She had a pleasant contralto voice, and she sounded very surprised. "Something about the house in Hollywood?—but it's through escrow now, I don't own it—what's this about? Well, yes, I'll be here all afternoon, but I don't—"

They picked up a quick sandwich at a coffee shop, and found the address in Monterey Park by a little after one. It was a sprawling stucco place with a red-tiled roof, on a street of groomed and middling expensive houses. And Mrs. Ogden was an attractive well-groomed woman in middle age, with graying brown hair, intelligent eyes, a figure only a little too plump. She looked at the L.A.P.D. badges with astonishment, but started to answer questions obediently.

The house on Ardmore had belonged to her father, Oliver Safford, but he hadn't lived in it for over twenty years before he died last March. It had been rented. He and her mother had lived in an apartment in Pasadena; her mother had died two years ago. "Dad left me the house, of course, and everything else, and we didn't want to bother with renting it, we put it on the market as soon as the will was through probate. I hadn't seen the place in over twenty years, and I don't suppose Dad had been near it in years, he wasn't driving the last five years — But what on earth's this all about, police asking—"

Rather obviously Joan Ogden or her deceased parent didn't have anything to do with the bodies, so Rodriguez told her, and she was horrified and interested. "Good Lord!" she said. "Good heavens. Of all the incredible things—"

"Do you have any record of the tenants there?"

"My heavens," she said. "Well, Dad kept all the records, I suppose on that as well as everything else—he was a stockbroker, you know, he kept records of everything—and the lawyer told us we'd better hang on to everything until the end of the year, for the tax people. There was a big box of papers, and his ledger—Ken put it all away in the den somewhere, I think—" She got up, and then said, "Wait a minute. I remember the name of the people who were living there when the house was sold, it was Orofino. They didn't want to move, and the lawyer had a little trouble with them. I'll have a look for that ledger—" She went down the hall leading from the living room, came back five minutes later and handed Rodriguez a big shabby old ledger, a large steel cash box. The ledger was nearly filled with precisely entered financial accounts in a neat copperplate. The box was filled with little bundles of papers secured with rubber bands.

"We'd like to have a close look at all this."

"Well, all right. But we'll need it all back for the tax accountant. My good heavens—that house. We'd told Dad he ought to have sold it years ago. It was the first house he and Mama bought—over forty years ago, they were living there when I was born—just after the war started. He was exempt from the draft because he was blind in one eye —he'd just started working for Stauffer and Chadwick, and of course we moved to Pasadena in 1949. He was making fairly good money, but he always said a nice little low-rental property was like a nest egg. All that part of Hollywood was starting to run down then—I was shocked when I saw the place again after he died. And Ken said it was really false economy, the place was rented for three-fifty but the taxes had gone up, of course, and the house was so old—not worth keeping up. But really, I can't get over this. Bodies buried there. Of all things. Ken's going to be absolutely fascinated—he's a mystery buff, you see."

They had just gotten back to the station and started to look at the records when a new call went down. D'Arcy and Nolan were questioning a suspect in an interrogation room down the hall, and nobody else was in. Resignedly, Rodriguez and Feinman went out on the new one. It was an address up on Outpost Drive. The householders, a Mr. and Mrs. Filey, had just gotten home from a ten-day vacation in Hawaii and discovered that they'd had a burglar. There was no telling when the burglar had hit, and at first glance it looked like a professional job.

"Damn it, there are good dead-bolt locks all around, I tried to take every precaution you're told about—" Filey was mad.

"They usually find a way," said Feinman, "if they're set on it. This sliding glass door—"

"Damn it, there's a lock on it, a special lock, it set me back—"

Feinman didn't tell him it had been a waste of money. The burglar had cut out a neat section of the sliding glass door onto the patio, enough to reach in and jimmy the lock. The patio wasn't overlooked by any neighbors. They'd get a lab man up here to dust for prints, but it had been a slick pro job; there probably wouldn't be any.

"Thank God I had all the good jewelry with me," said Mrs. Filey devoutly. "And my new coat—"

"My coin collection," said Filey savagely.

"I always said you ought to get a safe. Just leaving it in a box on the closet shelf—"

"We'd like a list of what's missing," said Rodriguez. "Have you got a record of the coins, sir?"

"Yes, sure, but there aren't any rarities—just British sovereigns and some American gold pieces—"

"I always said, a safe. And your tape recorder's gone, and the portable TV from the den—"

"Oh, hell!" said Filey. "My God, look at all this mess—"

The burglar usually left a mess, grabbing hurriedly for loot. Drawers had been dumped all over the house, pictures torn down, rugs yanked back—the pro burglar looking in all the expectable places.

"Have you got a record of the serial numbers on the recorder and TV?" asked Feinman.

Of course he hadn't. How many people wrote down serial numbers? He could give them brand names, that was all.

It was a little exercise in futility, taking nearly to the end of shift, and there'd be paperwork on it tomorrow. They left Franks dusting the master bedroom and got back to the office at five-thirty.

On Friday morning Sue and Maddox got to the station at the same time, a little late, and Sue went looking for Ellis. He was at his desk frowning over the night-watch report, running a hand through his thinning sandy hair. He'd taken on a little excess weight lately, and the rather loud plaid sports jacket looked tight across his beefy shoulders.

"The Truax woman," said Sue, "didn't make any mug shots, but

she's very positive on the description. Says she'd know him again anywhere. So maybe he's not in our records, but she agreed to a session
with an artist. Do you think it'd be worth the time?"

"Could be. Maybe it's his first time out, and a good composite sketch
—I'll set it up with headquarters if you want. See how busy they are
down there."

"I thought it might be worth a try."

"Sure." Ten minutes later he looked into the little office down the
hall. "There'll be an artist expecting you anytime, if you can get hold
of the witness."

Sue called Mrs. Truax, who said sure, she could spare the time.
"Any way I can help you catch these louts. Where do I go?"

"I'll take you down. Half an hour? Good, I'll expect you," said Sue
briskly.

Friday was Rodriguez' day off. Feinman had spread out all the
relevant rent receipts on Maddox's desk, and he and D'Arcy were
brooding over them when Maddox came back with a cup of coffee
from the machine.

"You can see how it shapes up, Ivor." Feinman shoved a little bundle of receipts across the desk. "At least there wasn't a stream of tenants in and out. Only two to think about. The house was rented to this
Arturo Orofino for the last couple of years—actually two and a half
years. The earliest date we've got here is four and a half years back,
and between then and the time Orofino moved in it was rented to a
Charles Hinman. We don't know how long before that he'd lived there.
Naturally, Safford being a very businesslike gent, by all his records, he
didn't keep receipts older than these."

"And damn it," said D'Arcy, "those bodies could have been there
longer than that, I suppose. But at least it's a place to start."

Maddox took a swallow of coffee and groped for a cigarette. "Why
and where?" he asked. "All right, Orofino having moved fairly recently, I suppose the post office will have a forwarding address. But
how the hell to locate this Hinman is something else. And we still don't
know a damned thing about the bodies. I hope the doctors can tell us
something—but there's no point in chasing around asking questions
until we do know something, is there? I should think Bergner could
give us something by tomorrow—my God, there wasn't much left of
the bodies to look at. But meanwhile, boys, something occurs to me
about that pair of heisters. By four good descriptions, it's the same pair

—both big, blond, in their twenties, big guns and so on. And I think there's something—mmh, funny about them."

"Funny how?" asked Feinman.

Maddox looked at his cigarette ruminatively. "Well, offbeat. Look at the places they've hit—hardly the usual places a heister would pick. A music store, a bowling alley, a dry cleaner's, for God's sake, and that old independent pharmacy on a side street. And there, they didn't take any drugs, didn't even ask for them. Even if the heister isn't a user himself, he knows the street value—it's as good as cash, the uppers and downers and whatever. And any idiot would know there wouldn't be much loot at those places. They didn't get much—twenty, thirty bucks."

"Looked at like that—so what could it say?"

"Could it be that they're new at the trade, nervous of hitting bigger places with more people around?"

D'Arcy made a derisive sound. "Amateurs? When they move in fast and didn't hesitate to take a shot at the pharmacist when he was a little slow opening the register?"

"I don't know," said Maddox. "They just strike me as offbeat." He shuffled the rent receipts like a pack of cards, put them all back into the steel box and shut it. "I suppose we'd get our heads bitten off if we called Bergner again. Damnation."

They were still kicking both of those around desultorily half an hour later when Lee Dowling came in with another of the possible suspects out of records. Feinman went to sit in on the questioning, and five minutes later a messenger came in with a big manila envelope.

It was the autopsy report on the Kelsey boy. Maddox scanned it rapidly and handed it over to D'Arcy. "Short and sweet," he said sadly. "Just the way we figured."

D'Arcy grimaced, reading it. "The wild animals in the jungle. Christ."

The Kelsey boy had been beaten up and sodomized. There were two cracked ribs, lacerations, burns on the lower body. He had died of a fractured skull, a blow from some fairly blunt weapon on the back of the head. The estimated time of death was between 5 and 9 P.M. last Tuesday night.

"Hell," said Maddox, taking it back to reread. "Things to do on this." He got up reluctantly; but as he reached for his coat, Baker looked into the office on his way back from the coffee machine, stirring dairy creamer into the paper cup.

"You'll get a report sometime. I just thought you'd like to know that we got damn all at that church. Lot of latents, good and bad, but nothing to say any of 'em belonged to the vandals. None of them in our records."

"Thank you so much," said Maddox. "We didn't really expect anything."

"Hell of a thing, those churches. I'm not much of a churchgoer, but those people are mostly peaceable souls minding their own business. It's got to be juveniles—ask me, Satan finding work for idle hands." Baker wandered on down the hall, and Maddox shrugged into his coat.

"We'd better take your car. Mine needs various things done to it, and if I'm going to go in for something new, no sense paying out the money. Unless I pass it on to Sue, and it's a toss-up whether it's any better than the Chrysler."

D'Arcy grunted, fishing out his keys. It was gray and threatening again today, still cold. They got into the Dodge in silence and D'Arcy started the engine. "You've been a little ray of sunshine lately," said Maddox. "What's the matter, had a fight with your best girl?"

"Mind your own business," said D'Arcy.

"I'll bet she found out what your name is, so you dropped her."

D'Arcy looked annoyed. And it wasn't, thought Maddox, really funny. D'Arcy was saddled with a very peculiar first name indeed, and he might have been the same man if he'd been christened Henry or John, but maybe not, too. As it was, he had them all trained never to mention it, and it was at least conceivable that the reason he was always changing girls was that he couldn't reasonably expect a girl to call him Hey-you all the time. It was an object lesson in a way, and one reason Maddox was putting his foot down about the names for the baby. Unthinkingly, parents could inflict a lot of psychic damage to offspring. He still remembered his impotent rage at that other fifth grader who had nicknamed him "Ivan the Terrible." It seemed a silly thing now but it hadn't been back then.

He lit a new cigarette, leaving D'Arcy in peace. D'Arcy was just between girls again.

Roy Kelsey opened the door to them after Maddox had pushed the bell twice. "Your boss told us you'd be home, Mr. Kelsey."

"Yeah. Nick said—take as much time as I needed. He's a good man. A good friend. I mean, you know, when there was only the two of us, Bobby and me—after Carol died—it just doesn't seem possible Bobby's gone too. Dead. All of a sudden like this." He turned away from the door, and they went in.

The apartment house on Loma Linda was middle-aged and middle-class, a little shabby. The living room here was comfortably enough furnished with old mismatched pieces; it looked a little dusty and neglected. Through an open arch at one end they could see into a rather bare little kitchen. There was a portable TV in one corner of this room.

"Just an accident," said Kelsey dully. "I don't understand it—he was always careful."

Maddox told him it hadn't been an accident; told him what it had been. Kelsey stared at them, and his apathy fell away; he seemed to swell, and his heavy shoulders hunched. He let loose a string of meaningless obscenities. "Oh, God, no, not like that—not that way—not Bobby! Why did it have to be Bobby? Oh, Christ—"

"We know how you feel, Mr. Kelsey, and we'd like to lay our hands on the man."

"God, if I ever got my hands on—" Kelsey was choking; he sat down on the shabby couch and put his head in his hands.

"You understand we have to ask questions." Kelsey nodded without looking up. "Did Bobby know enough to recognize one like that, do you think?"

Kelsey said roughly, "You think we hadn't warned him? Sure he knew better than to talk to any stranger—he was thirteen, a good sensible kid. He wouldn't have let the nut pick him up, any reason."

"All right," said D'Arcy. "As far as you knew, he went out after school to collect for his paper route?"

"Yeah, that's right. I wasn't so sure he ought to take a paper route, he had to get up damn early to make the deliveries—riding around on his bike—but he wanted to start earning, see. He'd had the route about six months, and he was getting to be a regular good little businessman —receipt book with carbon and all. It was just close around here, mostly above the boulevard—oh, my God, could it have been one of them?" He looked up wildly.

"He was on a bike?" They hadn't heard that before. And there hadn't been a receipt book on him. "What kind of bike?"

"It's an old three-speed—I couldn't afford a new one—it's a Schwinn, green and white—"

"Would he have had a list of the people he delivered to?"

"I don't know. Maybe. We could look—his room—"

It was the usual boy's room, a single bed with a plain brown spread, a worn rug, scarred chest of drawers, a few books in a cheap bookcase, a small student desk. It was in the top drawer of the desk that Maddox found a single folded sheet of notebook paper with a list of names and addresses written in a careful round childish hand. There were twenty-eight names. The addresses went from Russell Avenue in the next block to Franklin, Oxford Place, Winona, Kingsley—a few farther down below Hollywood Boulevard.

"He couldn't get to all of them in one day, he usually took two or three days collecting every month. And I always told him, be home before dark. . . . No, I've got no idea where he'd start collecting—I just don't know. Oh, Christ, why should it happen to Bobby? Why?" Suddenly, Kelsey's face contorted and he began to cry, as openly and unashamedly as a child.

Sometimes the legwork was the only way to do it. It was early afternoon before they hit Bobby's trail. At the seven addresses above Franklin where somebody was at home, nobody had seen Bobby on Tuesday. At the first address they tried on Russell, he had collected the month's subscription money at about three-thirty. At the next two addresses, on Serrano, he'd been there a little later.

A Mrs. Jacobson on Hobart, below the boulevard, said he'd been there about four-fifteen. "He's usually a reliable kid, but maybe he's been sick, hasn't brought the paper the last couple of days." She didn't seem curious why they were asking. He had had two more subscribers on that block, but neither of them was home. There were only two more down here, both on Harvard, a block away. "Collecting from the ones farthest away first," said D'Arcy.

"It looks like it." It hadn't started to rain yet, but the sky was threatening and dark.

Both addresses on Harvard were in an old double court, three duplexes on each side of a middle walk, with a row of single garages at the back. Mrs. Ortiz, in the left rear unit, said the boy had come by about a quarter past five on Tuesday, she'd told him to stop the paper, her husband said it was too expensive and you got the news on radio and TV anyways. At the left front unit a motherly-looking Mrs. Ostermeyer told them that Bobby had been there about five-thirty. "Why you asking? I been worried maybe he's sick, he hasn't brought the paper since—he's a nice boy—it was getting dark then, I said he shouldn't ought to be out so late, wouldn't want one of mine out after dark, and he said he was heading straight home then. He went riding his bike up toward the street— What you asking for? Was there an accident, did he get hurt?"

"That's right," said Maddox. "He got hurt."

"Oh, that's terrible—I'm sorry."

Starting back to the street, D'Arcy said, "So he'd be going just a block up to the boulevard, and another block over to Loma Linda. On the bike, about ten minutes."

"And where's the bike? He was dumped in that alley off Sunset, six blocks away. He was taken there in a car."

"Had to be. And it was a rainy night," said D'Arcy. "Getting dark. Did anybody see anything?"

"We go ringing doorbells and ask. And we'd better start right here."

They would have to come back to the court, being thorough; there were only two other people at home. A Miss Harmer in the left middle unit said she took the *Times* and hadn't seen any newsboy around on Tuesday afternoon. At the front unit opposite Mrs. Ostermeyer's door, where a name slot on the mailbox said SNELL, a little black woman told them she hadn't been home on Tuesday till ten o'clock, and her son had been out too.

As they came out to the street it began to rain gently.

Adeline Truax had a long session with the police artist at headquarters downtown, patiently studying the Identikit pages and picking out face shapes, mouths, hairlines, eyebrows and ears. In the end the artist came up with a composite sketch that satisfied her. "That's him to a T, that sort of low forehead and wide cheeks and the way his ears stuck out. I'd swear to him any day. I didn't see the other one so close, this was the one did the talking, and shoved the gun right at me. Say, you're a real good artist. You got him down just right."

They ran off a batch of photocopies. Sue drove her back to Hollywood and thanked her, and passed the copies around.

Feinman studied one interestedly. "Kind of face you might remember, I can see—he looks like a low-life lout all right. But when nobody made a mug shot, what can we do with this?"

"Hand one to every squad," said Daisy. "Somebody might spot him."

It was after one and Sue was starving, but just then a new call came in: reported child molestation. Technically they had a Juvenile bureau here, two policewomen and an older sergeant, but at the moment they were all downtown testifying in court.

"You go and have lunch," said Daisy. "Eating for two as they say. Joe can go with me."

Bill Nolan, at the next desk, who looked even younger than his twenty-six years, fair and slender, was still looking relieved when they all drifted out.

Ken Donaldson and Dick Brougham had been sitting on night watch for a good long time; they were both amiable souls and just as glad to have somebody new to talk to. Roger Stacey had put in seven years as a detective at Hollenbeck station; he was stocky and blue-chinned, nakedly bald at thirty-five, and he always had some new snapshots of his six kids to show. He kidded the other two about being bachelors.

"Listen, if either of us got married," Brougham was always telling him, "we'd have to go back on day watch, and I don't remember how to sleep at night anymore."

When they came on, at eight on Friday night, there was a teletype centered on Maddox's desk. "What the hell is this about?" asked Donaldson, picking it up. "From the Houston boys—somebody wants a body sent down there. Who's Livesey? Well, it's the day watch's business, let them worry."

Friday night was sometimes busy, the start of the weekend, but they didn't get a call until nine-forty. The Traffic man said it looked like a mugging, and the woman was dead.

"Curson Street," said Brougham. "That seems to ring a little bell— we had a mugging up around there, sometime last week, it was a fellow named Smith or Johnson or something—"

"Brown," said Donaldson. "I wrote the report. He got jumped when he went to open the garage door, coming home. He wasn't much hurt, knocked out for a couple of minutes—the mugger got his wallet but there wasn't much in it."

He and Stacey went out on it. The rain had stopped, but more was forecast. Up on that narrow dark street above Hollywood Boulevard they found Patrolman Stoner and an agitated middle-aged couple named Conklin. A few feet away on the sidewalk was a huddled dark heap.

"We found her," burst out Mrs. Conklin as they came up. "He said to wait for the detectives, are you the detectives? He said she's *dead*— we were coming home from our daughter's and when Fred turned in the drive the headlights— It's Esther Cook! She lives two houses up— he said she's *dead!* Such a nice woman—her poor sister—she just gave me all those geranium slips—" She was crying thinly.

"I guess somebody ought to go tell her sister," said Conklin. "Mrs. Eisenberg. She's a widow, they live together, Miss Cook never got married. When we found her, I called in right away but we must've waited a good half hour before the patrol car came—" Neither of them was much enamored of Patrolman Stoner. "I couldn't believe she was dead, but he wouldn't call a ambulance—"

Stoner turned his back on them and said confidentially, "Look, it's Johnny McCrea's beat but he was out on Code Seven, they had to chase me over—I was way out on La Brea. She was still warm. These people must have spotted her just a few minutes after she was attacked. She's dead all right, and there's no sign of a handbag."

"Ergo, a mugging," said Stacey. He squatted over the huddled form on the sidewalk and Stoner directed his flashlight on it.

She was facedown, knees bent, her right arm flung out above her head. "Read it," said Donaldson. "He came on her from behind, and hit hard—too hard. She cracked her skull on the sidewalk, probably passed out instantly." There wasn't any blood visible. Stacey gently raised the head and turned it. She hadn't been young, but in the glare of the flashlight it was a regular-featured pleasant face. She'd been wearing a little knitted cap, bright green; it had slipped halfway off her head, and her hair was ash-blond, probably tinted. She was indubitably dead: no pulse.

"You ought to tell Mrs. Eisenberg—it isn't right, just leave her lying there—I didn't believe she was dead, but he said— And what was she doing out here? She's got her own car—"

"We'll want you to come in and make a statement," said Stacey. "You didn't see anybody else on the street, anybody running away?"

"No, there wasn't a soul. My God, I thought that patrol car would never come. They say we got a good force—I don't know—" Conklin cast a baleful glance at Stoner, leading his wife up their front walk.

The house two doors up was a modest gray stucco, with a porch light shining on a minute front porch. Mrs. Eisenberg was a slim gray-haired woman in a tailored navy housecoat; she listened to them numbly. She said, "I'd been worried—she should have been home half an hour ago —I tried to call, but of course the shop was closed. Adele's Boutique —on Sunset—where Esther works. Her car was in the garage, since Wednesday—she had to take the bus. Usually they close at six, but they're open to nine on Friday—only Mrs. Willing said she could leave early, because of getting the bus. I worried about her walking home in the dark—oh, you can't be saying Esther's dead—she's ten years younger than me, only fifty-two—"

They did all the indicated things, and called up a morgue wagon. There'd be a report to type, and that would probably be the end of it.

Stoner said unresentfully, "Damn it, the citizens didn't appreciate me much, did they? I got here as soon as I could."

"The citizens don't always appreciate us," said Donaldson wryly.

CHAPTER 3

Johnny McCrea had been taking his Code Seven—out for lunch—at a little bar on Fairfax. He wasn't supposed to be going into a bar on duty, but he wasn't having a drink, of course, just a sandwich and coffee.

The little bar had been there for a long time, a neighborhood place called Benny's, with the usual casual neighborhood clientele until a couple of months ago. One day—the story had gotten around since—the owner had been approached by a big fat black man who offered him a proposition. "Me and the other boys, like they say oldies but still goodies, and we miss playin' for the people. You let us play, nobody likes us you don't have to pay." There was a minute platform and a tiny dance floor, unused for years, and a piano. The little combo of four men, two white and two black, turned up the next night, and about the only comment the owner got in the next week was from a young truck driver who said those guys sure played a lot of old stuff, didn't they. But the night after that, the music critic for the *Herald* had a flat tire in the parking lot three doors up and dropped into the bar while he waited for the auto-club truck. The result was a lyrical review spread all over his half page in the entertainment section.

"Your correspondent couldn't believe his aging eyes and ears at first, but there they are, folks, some of the best out of the great big-band era. You aficionados past forty, well, call it fifty, you remember big Claude 'Cloudy' Delarue, for how many years the star of Howie Hallett's Mellow Music Makers, and little Artie Robson from the same outfit—and Briny Nelson on drums and marimba, Pete Parris and his nimble fiddle, from Bob Daly's sounds of sweet swing—remember? There they are as big as life, and still the best we ever had with us, for the blues and swing and jazz and a little of the sweet stuff. Delarue still handles the sweetest tenor sax this side of heaven, and Artie hasn't forgotten how to hit the ivories. Old Cloudy may admit to seventy-eight, but there's nothing amiss with his musical know-how. 'Man,' he told me, 'don't try to tell me this Godawful gut-howling gets called music really sends most of the people, except the poor kids who don't know better. We're has-beens maybe, sittin' around drawing the pensions—we all knew each other from the old days—we happened to meet up at Howie Hallett's funeral last month, got to talkin'. And we all missed playing for the people, you know what I mean. The audiences. Just thought we'd like to see if the people still like us, if we're still on the upbeat.' Well, folks, the boys are still on the upbeat, and any of you nostalgia buffs who appreciate the oldies superbly performed by the real artists, drop into Benny's, sit back and enjoy!"

The review had changed the clientele at the little bar somewhat drastically. It was the latest "in" place now for the quiet and respectable upper-class crowd; it was packed the four nights a week the little combo played. The owner, somewhat astonished, did some redecorating, renamed the place The Blue Note, with a new neon sign over the door, and sat back to reap the profits. There was also a second bartender and short-order chef, with a classier menu.

McCrea had been a blues and swing buff since his high school days, and since he'd been transferred to this shift last month he usually dropped in here for his Code Seven. The combo was very damn good, all right. He had finished his sandwich and was thinking about another cup of coffee—that piercing-sweet tenor sax was giving out with some pretty fancy improvisations on "Sweet Georgia Brown"—when he woke up and looked at his watch. He'd been out forty minutes, too long. He hurried out into the cold damp night and checked in on the radio.

"Where the hell have you been?" asked the dispatcher. "There's a call. Unknown trouble, Las Palmas."

"O.K., I'm on it," said McCrea.

The address was up above Franklin, an old California bungalow, and there was a distracted woman waiting for him, a Mrs. Beecher. "We've got to find her!" she told him. "My God, the stupid things kids do—and my husband's out of town for the company, if only he was home, but I couldn't leave Pam—" There was a little girl about eight or nine there on the front porch with her, looking sulky. "It's Jean Fisher—Pam's best friend—she was sleeping over, they were listening to records in Pam's room. And I was at the back of the house doing the laundry—when I went to settle them in bed Jean was gone, they'd had a silly spat over something and she said she was going home—of all the stupid things, Pam should have told me right away—"

The little girl said, "It's only a couple of blocks."

"I called Mrs. Fisher, and Jean's not home—must be an hour ago—

she's in bed with flu and I told her not to go out in this cold, I'd call you—we've got to find her! Well, they live down on Yucca—anything could have happened, we've got to—"

McCrea, cruising down the little dark streets looking, found Jean Fisher half an hour later. He found her crumpled up against the curb at the corner of Yucca and Whitley. Her tan quilted coat was covered with mud and her skull was smashed where she'd been hit and thrown against the curb. She had probably been killed instantly.

McCrea had been riding a squad for nearly two years, and he'd seen death too often before, and had to break the bad news, but he'd never get to enjoy it.

On Saturday morning, with Feinman off, they drifted in more or less at the same time, and Ellis perched a hip on the corner of Maddox's desk, watching him read the night-watch report. The night watch had only had two calls, but both were homicides.

Maddox handed the report to D'Arcy, and Rodriguez read it over his shoulder.

"Damn all!" said Maddox. "There'll be nothing to get on that mugging, he wouldn't have meant to kill the woman. The sister says she might have had ten dollars on her. And the little girl's an obvious hit-run."

Rodriguez said sadly, "Nine years old. Poor little devil. Starting home after a little spat with the girl friend. The lab may turn up something from the clothes."

"I just wish," said D'Arcy, "there was somewhere definite to go on the Kelsey boy, damn it."

"Oh, for God's sake," said Maddox, "you know as well as I do, there are too many places to look." They could ring more doorbells and ask, but it was very doubtful that anybody had seen anything of Bobby Kelsey and his killer that late dark afternoon. If they were going to get anything on it, it would be the hard way. Look in records for the known sex offenders with the suggestive pedigrees, bring them in and question them. That kind were sometimes spooky, and the right X might come out with a confession. They had put Bobby's green bicycle on the pawnbrokers' hot list, but it was just an anonymous bike, they hadn't even a model number on it.

D'Arcy said, "That area—we can't even pin it down closer by picking the nuts with local addresses. A block down, a block up from Hollywood Boulevard, and along there the nut could blend into the crowd of different nuts, all the porno stores and movie houses."

"Isn't it the truth," said Maddox. "But I don't know, D'Arcy. The boy could have been spotted by the nut, on his way home crossing the boulevard, and up on those quiet residential streets at that hour, nobody to see the nut grab him. But—"

"The nut in a car?" asked Rodriguez. "You said the kid wouldn't let a stranger con him, had been warned about perverts—"

"How do we know what happened? It could be he was just pounced on from behind, he wouldn't be strong enough to fight a grown man, César. But he must have been tortured and killed somewhere right around there, because of where he was dumped, only a few blocks from where he was picked up."

"In an apartment or a house," said D'Arcy. "Or the car."

"And the sooner we get to the legwork the better. Try a first cast out of our records, maybe we'll turn lucky." Maddox and D'Arcy went up to the records office, and in the hall Sue blundered past them at a run, making for the rest rooms. Daisy, in the doorway of the small office, said to Maddox, "Your wife's just discovered she's going to have morning sickness after all. Don't fuss, Ivor, it's a natural phenomenon and probably won't last long."

There was quite a list of sex offenders in Hollywood's records, even when they weeded out the least likely ones, concentrating on the ones who liked little boys, had records of incipient violence. They shared the job and by ten-thirty had compiled a list of thirty-three names. "Probabilities," said D'Arcy, looking at it. "Try the close-in addresses first?"

"There's never an easy shortcut," said Maddox sardonically. "The killer could live in Santa Monica and have a like-minded pal with a pad a block off the boulevard."

They wanted as many hands on this as possible, and went back to the detective office to see who was still in. They found Dr. Bergner talking to Ellis and Rodriguez. As usual the pudgy little doctor was smoking a long black cigar.

He waved it at the other two. "I was just saying, we had a look at your two old corpses. It's a damned queer thing, in a couple of ways. We can tell you this and that, but I can't see that it'll take you very far. To begin with, they're both female. There's no indication how they died, no obvious injuries. Could have been strangled or poisoned, they're both too far gone to show anything. We took X rays of the skeletons, and they were both mature adults, but that gives you quite a leeway, of course. As to how long they'd been there, well, that's damn difficult to say. All I can offer you is a rough estimate. I'd say one of them is older than the other—as a corpse that is. That one might have been buried from three to four years, the other one maybe two or three. That one had on what was left of a few clothes, we sent them to the lab downtown—don't know if they'll make anything out of them. And that's about it."

"Well, thanks for small favors," said Rodriguez.

"If you ever find out anything about them, let me know—I'd be interested," said Bergner. He left the stub of his cigar smoldering in Maddox's ashtray and took himself off.

And knowing what the doctors could say about those bodies, there were things to do on that. Nolan and Dowling were both in, and Maddox divided the list of sex offenders with them. He and D'Arcy started out to look for the name at the top of the list—Alfred Berger, last known address Council Street, pedigree of child molestation, assault with intent and enticement of minors.

Rodriguez went out to see what he could discover about the tenants in the Ardmore Street house.

Not, he reflected, that it would be easy to find out anything about the bodies, by the little they knew. But Rodriguez always enjoyed the offbeat cases. So they had the names of the latest tenants, occupying that house up to four and a half years ago, it might not mean one damned thing relevant to the bodies. According to the rent receipts, the house had been vacant for about two months after Charles Hinman had moved out. The doctors, damn their confident pronouncements, couldn't be entirely sure just how long the bodies had been dead and buried, even that one was older than the other—Bergner admitted it was an educated guess. They could have been stashed away there together, when the house was vacant. Or even before Hinman had lived there, and they didn't know how long he'd been there, or who had lived there before that. In fact, it was doubtful that they'd ever find out anything about those bodies, but they could go through a few motions.

Rodriguez tried the local post office on Vermont and asked about Arturo Orofino. The Orofinos had just moved out of the house in August, after living there for about twenty-eight months, and the post office had a forwarding address: Burns Avenue. Rodriguez found it, another shabby old frame house on a tired shabby street. He found Mrs. Carmen Orofino at home, with four small children underfoot. Her English wasn't too good and she was pleased when he switched to Spanish. He had made up a tale to explain his questions, but he didn't need it; she was voluble. She was comfortably fat, with masses of dark hair and a beautiful milky complexion, and it took only a mention of the Ardmore Street address to set her off. It had been, she told him, a terrible big nuisance, the people making them move out, just because that house got sold, it was a good house, and the rent not so bad either, they couldn't find a house the same size for the same rent. "You can see for yourself"—and she gestured broadly—"all the kids, the other three are in school, and that house had three bedrooms, we only got two here, and sometimes I take care of my sister's four kids too—and Arturo and I both got families here, there's no room when people come to visit, but rents are just terrible now—but you were saying about that house on Ardmore, mister, you think maybe we could get it back?"

Rodriguez, envisioning vast crowds of Orofinos and in-laws, an unspecified number of small children—talk about a cloud of witnesses —decided that there couldn't possibly have been sufficient privacy to bury one or both of the bodies during their tenancy. And Bergner said one of the bodies might have been dead up to four years. "No, I'm afraid not," he said, preparing retreat. "I'm trying to find a Mrs. Lopez, who lived in the apartment next door, did you know her?"

She lost interest. "We never knew any of the neighbors around there."

Back in the car, he ruminated. Ardmore Street was in a working-class neighborhood. Not the kind of street where settled residents might know their neighbors. Apartment houses on both sides of that old house. But there wasn't anywhere else to look. He drove over there, and parked in front of where that house had been. All the rubble was cleared away now, the garage knocked down, the grass and bushes left in the yard plowed under, and the lot was ready for the nice new apartment to be built. The apartments on either side looked jerry-built and garish with too-bright color.

He tried the one on the left first. He found only one woman home, an elderly woman who was annoyed at him for interrupting her soap opera. She said she'd lived there only a year and didn't know any of the neighbors. At the other apartment he found three women at home; none of them had ever known anyone who lived in the house between.

They could ask the night watch to get back to all the tenants here, but he doubted if any of them would have any information. It was a transient neighborhood. He went back to the car and stood there on the sidewalk, lighting a cigarette and looking at the empty lot, thinking about those bodies. There just wasn't anywhere else to go. By now, the post office wouldn't have a record of a forwarding address, and all they knew about Hinman was his name.

A battered pickup truck pulled in behind the Ford, and a nonde-script man got out of it and started to unload a lawn mower from the truck bed. He looked at Rodriguez incuriously, trundled the mower up the sidewalk to the strip of grass in front of the apartment next door. Rodriguez went after him.

"Excuse me, have you been doing the yard work here for long?"

"Little there is to do, mow the lawn, trim the bushes. About six years, why?" He was a medium-sized man about forty, with bulging muscles.

"I'm looking for a man who used to live in the house that was here, the lot next door. A Charles Hinman. Would you know anything about him?" It was a very outside chance.

"Oh," said the gardener. "Oh, yeah, I remember that guy. Vaguely. It must be about four years back, I was here one day and he came over and asked me what to do about aphids, they were eating his roses. I told him a spray to get. I wouldn't have remembered that, a'course he didn't mention his name then, but it was funny, just a couple weeks later he sold me a pair of shoes."

"How do you mean, a pair of shoes?"

"Well, I needed some, I went into the store on account there was a sale, and he was the salesman waited on me. That was the only time I heard his name. Hadn't thought of it again till you said it. You a private eye?"

"No," said Rodriguez. "What store was it?"

"That big chain—Lester's. Over on Highland."

Rodriguez thanked him warmly, got into the Ford and went looking for the nearest pay phone where there'd be a phone book.

Maddox and D'Arcy felt as if they'd wasted the day, but that was how some days went. They had just, at five-twenty, finished a session with one of the sex offenders; he had a reasonably good alibi and they let him go. He was only the second one they'd found to talk to. Five others had moved, no one knew where, and none of the rest were at home, and none of their neighbors knew if or where they worked. Alfred Berger had had an alibi too; he worked at a porno movie house from one to nine, and five people had said he'd been there all Tuesday.

It was the hard way to go at it, and they were tired. They hadn't seen Nolan or Dowling since this morning.

Rodriguez came in looking pleased with himself. "I ran into a little luck," he said, and told them about the gardener. "It was a store on

Highland, the other side of Sunset. Hinman was assistant manager there, up to two years ago last May."

"Thirty months," said Maddox sleepily. "That's when he moved out of the house on Ardmore."

"Yes," said Rodriguez, "and now we know why. He got transferred to another Lester's store. Promoted to manager at a store in Long Beach. There's just one clerk still at the store here who knew him, the current manager came in after he left. The clerk's worked there for about four years, and Hinman was there then. He thinks Hinman hadn't been there long at the time. But this is where connections start to break down." Rodriguez sat back and smoothed his mustache thoughtfully.

"Why?" asked D'Arcy.

"He was all upset because police were asking questions. He's a rabbity little fellow, all very gentlemanly, and he told me Mr. Hinman's a very quiet, steady, respectable man, what could police want of him, he'd never had anything to do with the police. I let him think we were looking for an innocent witness, and I got a description out of him." Rodriguez lit a cigarette and contemplated it. "All I can say is, Mr. Charles Hinman certainly doesn't sound like the type to leave the mysterious dead bodies behind. He was between forty-five and fifty then, about five-five, a little too fat, nearly bald and he wears glasses, he's nearsighted. A very neat dresser. He doesn't smoke or drink and he's something of a health-food nut."

"No, he doesn't sound very exciting," agreed Maddox. "But we'd like to talk to him. Is he married? Any family?"

"None ever mentioned that the clerk heard about. And the only thing a little queer about that is, if he's all alone why did he rent a whole house? But of course by what that gardener said, maybe he likes the yard work, and that was why." Rodriguez reached for the appropriate phone book and started looking. "He'd have moved down there to be closer to the new job, and that was two and a half years ago, he ought to be listed— Condenación. With a vengeance. There are three of them—C. Hinman and two Charleses."

"It's a big town," said Maddox. "Go look tomorrow, César. Personally, I'm ready to go home." Sue had already left, saying she was still feeling queasy. "Back to the grind in the morning—the legwork won't go away."

When he got home to the old house on Starview Terrace, in the full dark, the big Akita came to greet him amiably at the back door. Tama was reasonably fond of both the Maddoxes, but as far as he was concerned Margaret was head of the household; he was seldom far away from her. Maddox would feel a good deal easier, his two females home alone after the baby arrived, with the savage-looking monster around.

Margaret was busy with something at the stove. "Sue's lying down, but I'll get her up for dinner."

"Is she all right? Maybe she ought to see the doctor again—"

"Don't be silly, Ivor. She'll be fine. I just hope this stage doesn't last long. I was sick as a dog the first month with her, but the rest of the time I never felt better."

"Well, if you're sure—"

"I'm sure. You look tired—get yourself a drink, sit down and relax." She gave him a fond smile.

"It's very nice to have a grandmother to come home to," said Maddox.

The night watch came on expecting a busy night. Saturday night was the night for the denizens of the jungle to go on the tear. When the front desk sent up a call at nine-thirty, Brougham said, "Here we go, boys." Stacey went out with him, and shivered involuntarily as they got out to the parking lot.

"Damn, it must be nearly down to freezing. I don't remember this cold a winter in years." And the forecasters were still predicting more rain.

The address was close in on Melrose; it was a block of old stores, all dark and closed except for one in the middle of the block, where the squad was parked. Brougham pulled up in front. Stoner was waiting for them in the doorway.

"Join the force and have fun. You've got another homicide."

"So you'd better call up the lab," said Stacey.

"I don't think they'd get anything, by what the lady says. It sounds like a kind of accidental thing," said Stoner. "She owns the place. Mrs. Siegel. The dead man was Robert Pike. Retired widower on a pension."

The sign over the door said HARRIET'S PET SHOP. They all went in. It was a small place, hardly thirty feet square; there was a counter with a cash register on it along the left-side wall, and shelves at the back and the other side. At this end of the counter a man was sprawled on the floor, his eyes staring-wide up at the fluorescent ceiling light. He was a fairly big, bald old man, and a bulky overcoat was splayed out on either side of him. The woman was huddled on a high stool behind the counter, a big rawboned middle-aged woman with rather wild hennaed hair.

"Mrs. Siegel," said Stoner. "Here are the detectives, ma'am."

"Can you tell us what happened here?" asked Brougham.

She wet her lips. "They held us up," she said huskily. "Two men. I was just closing—at nine o'clock. Sometimes I get customers on a Saturday night, stay open. Mr. Pike—we live in the same apartment house round on Sycamore, he's a nice old man, always came to walk me home, said I shouldn't be out alone. Business been slow all day—only money I took in, for those last two pups."

"Two men held you up?" asked Stacey.

"AWK! Hello, hello, good-bye, have a nice day!" The raucous gleeful voice was loud, right behind them, and Brougham and Stacey jumped around, startled. The big red and green parrot was perched in the front shop window; it chuckled obscenely and winked at them. "My God," said Brougham.

Mrs. Siegel gave a little dry sob. "That's Caruso," she said. "It was his fault. They came in—we were just ready to leave—I don't know why they'd think there was much money here. I only asked five apiece for the pups, they were just mutts. And they both had guns, one of them said this is a stickup, lady—and I guess we were both more surprised than scared—I started to open the register—and then Caruso squawked—just like he did now—and it must have scared the fellow, not expecting it, and he jumped and the gun went off—and they just ran out without taking anything—"

"I'll be damned," said Stacey. He went to look at the dead man. Accidental or not, the slug had gotten him squarely over the heart, by the blood on his shirt. "Now this is a queer one, Dick."

"AWK! Hello, hello! Have a nice day, dear!" The parrot extended its wings exuberantly, "Good-bye! Have a nice day, dear!"

There wasn't much to do but call up a morgue wagon, go back and write a report on it. And out in the streets the squads might be having a busy night, with the drunks and muggers and stolen cars, but that was the only call the night watch had the entire shift.

Ellis and Daisy were off on Sunday, and Sue had decided to stay home. Maddox was a little worried about her, but Margaret said she'd be all right.

There was still a long list of sex offenders to go hunting, and so far they were looking only for the locals. Records downtown would give them twenty times the number, if they decided to ask.

He looked over the night report without sitting down and said, "For God's sake." He thrust it at Feinman. They were all standing around waiting to lay out the day, except D'Arcy, who had wandered down the hall after coffee; he was never operating on all cylinders in the early morning.

"A pet store, for the love of God!" said Maddox. "Attempted heist at a pet store! Not even one of the classy ones with the pedigreed pups —little hole in the wall out on Melrose selling birdseed and cat litter! The village idiot would know there wouldn't be any loot there. And by this description the Siegel woman gave Dick, that was our offbeat pair. Scared by a parrot and accidentally firing the gun! And not a sign of the slug anywhere, Dick thinks it went right through the old man and out into the street. She's supposed to come in to make a statement—so we show her that composite sketch, and she'll say that's him. Want to bet?"

"No bets," said Feinman. "It's the same funny combination, they're fast and experienced but—offbeat."

"And I think it's about time we got this description on the wire to NCIC," said Maddox. "We know they're not in our records—the Truax woman at least would have spotted a mug shot. So they may be in somebody else's."

"I'll go along with that," agreed Feinman, rubbing his jaw. "I'll go do it." He started down the hall for Communications.

Rodriguez hadn't taken his coat off. "I'm going down to Long Beach after Hinman. Wish me luck. And do have fun with the sex fiends."

Dowling and Nolan went out with their half of the list, and Maddox was just reaching for his coat to start out with D'Arcy when the phone rang on his desk. "Oh, no," he said.

"Sunday morning. It'll be another church getting vandalized," said D'Arcy.

"Maddox. What now?"

Whitwell said, "No rest for the wicked, Sergeant. Traffic just called in a homicide. For once you'll be meeting some respectable rich people. At least rich. It's Mulholland Drive."

"Give me the address," said Maddox resignedly.

When Feinman came back from Communications the office was empty. Well, somebody ought to stay in to mind the store. He sat down at his desk and lit a cigarette. He thought for a while about what to get his wife for her birthday next week, but didn't come to any conclusion. He thought about those buried bodies; like Rodriguez, he was rather fascinated by those bodies, but he didn't think it was very likely they were going to unravel that one in a hurry. The Kelsey boy was, you could say, more immediate. At least there was a chance to drop on that one, if it involved a hell of a lot of legwork. At least a chance to drop on some of the heisters. But the way it so often happened, the rest of what they had to work was just shapeless, with no handles at all. That hit-run, and the woman killed by the mugger, most of the heists, the long list of burglaries.

A man appeared in the doorway and stood there hesitantly. "Is this the detective office? The guy out in front said to come back here and see a detective."

"Yes, sir. What can we do for you?" asked Feinman.

"Well, it's about a murder," said the man nervously.

"Oh," said Feinman. "Well, come in and sit down."

He was a medium-sized man about forty-five, with thin brown hair and a little paunch. He had a homely bulldog face without any eyebrows, and his nose had been broken at least once. He was wearing a dirty blue shirt and wrinkled tan pants. He sat down in the chair beside Feinman's desk and said, "Well, it's—well, I want to confess to a murder. It's been on my conscience a long time, and the way I been feeling—I think maybe there's something wrong with me, like, you know, in my head. Maybe I oughta see a head doctor." His eyes were anxious.

Feinman said gently, "You committed a murder? Would you like to tell me your name?"

"Sure," said the man readily. "Sure. My name's Charles Dickens. It was about eighteen years ago, I killed this woman outside a bar over on Third Street. Her name was Marion. I hit her on the head with a brick. I didn't mean to kill her, I don't know why I did."

Charles Dickens. Eighteen years ago, a woman named Marion. Feinman sighed and shut his eyes briefly. Just another nut.

When Cassidy pulled up at the address the dispatcher had given him, he was surprised to see it was a church, and then he knew what he was going to see. He had been called out to two of the other ones, a couple of weeks ago.

This was a little place on Gower, an old frame building with a modest sign on the front: GOSPEL LIGHT COMMUNITY CHURCH. The two men waiting for him at the front door were both fairly elderly and much agitated.

Cassidy looked, and it was the same goddamned mess as the others had been. The spray paint, the obscenities, the Bible torn apart. There was a back window broken. He went back to the squad and called the front office, but after a delay the dispatcher told him there didn't seem to be any detectives available. They'd be hearing about it sometime.

Cassidy didn't know what the detectives could do about it anyway. The damned mindless juveniles. Satan finding work for idle hands.

The house on Mulholland Drive was a big two-story Spanish place with a red-tiled roof, not a new house but solidly handsome. It sat on a corner of the curving street with extensive lawn front and sides. All of this area was redolent of money—not the new splashy show-biz money, but the respectable old substantial kind. There was a curved brick walk up to a tiled porch and carved double front doors. The Traffic man waiting for them there was Ramon Gonzales, as tall and dark as D'Arcy and a good deal broader.

"So, a quick rundown," said Maddox.

"Householder shot," said Gonzales. "His name's Charles Mainwaring. The maid found him when she came to set the table for breakfast, noticed a light still on in his study. He's about fifty-five, sixty. I'd say he was shot some time last night, and there's no sign of a gun. It was the maid's night out—her name's Amy Dobson—and the wife was out too, they both got in around eleven. Didn't hear anything."

"And the wife never looked in on him to say, 'I'm home,' didn't notice he never came to bed?" Maddox sniffed. "Well, I trust you kept them away from any evidence."

"Don't insult me, Sergeant. The scene's preserved."

Maddox and D'Arcy went into the entrance hall, wide and red-tiled. "Straight down to the right," said Gonzales; but Maddox stopped to look into the living room immediately on the left, a vast rectangular room crowded with furniture. There were two women in there, staring back at him fearfully. It was obvious which was which. The maid was in the semi-uniform of a blue cotton housedress; she was fat and gray-haired, with a round face innocent of makeup. She looked more excited than scared. The other woman was younger if maybe not by much, and she wasn't wearing makeup either; she'd evidently just gotten out of bed, was wearing a fleecy wine-colored robe and velvet slippers to match. Her ash-blond hair was professionally groomed, her nails tinted a deep pink. She was a very good-looking woman, a triangular kitten face, wide-set blue eyes.

"Mrs. Mainwaring," he said, and she nodded jerkily at him. "We'll want to talk to you in a little while, if you feel up to it."

"May I—go up and get dressed?" she asked a little thickly. Her voice was low and pleasant.

"Well, if you'll just be patient a little while, please."

"But you ought to call Mr. Jim," said the maid. "It's only right he should know. And the lawyer."

"There'll be time, Amy. Later. I suppose—they know what they're doing."

Gonzales would see the women stayed put. Maddox and D'Arcy went down the hall and found the study.

It was a room at least twenty feet square, and everything in it said money, but in an unostentatious whisper. The mahogany desk was massive, the leather-upholstered chairs were deep and there was a fireplace with a marble mantel. The dark-brown carpet was thick underfoot.

Even the dead man looked like money. He was sitting in the tall-backed desk chair, a little slumped to one side. He was a big man with very distinctive features, a big high-bridged nose looking arrogant even in death, square clean-shaven jaw, tufted eyebrows, close-cut gray hair still plentiful. He was fully dressed in a sharply tailored gray suit, white shirt and discreet charcoal-gray tie. There was a small black-brown mark just above his left temple.

"Small caliber," said Maddox. "And no exit wound—the slug's still in him." He didn't need the lab to tell him it had been nearly a contact wound: there were powder burns in the gray hair, around the little hole. And no gun on the scene.

On the opulent leather-bound blotter on the desk lay a single sheet of paper and a pen. Nothing else on the desk but a telephone. Maddox looked at the sheet over the dead man's shoulder. It bore a severely modern letterhead: MAINWARING MANAGEMENT AND INVESTMENT, INC., an address on Sunset nearly into West Hollywood. There were just three words written under that, in a firm plain script—*My dear Sanford*—and a dash.

D'Arcy said, "There's one of these patent locks on the door." There was a sliding glass door looking out on a side yard, a little manicured rose garden.

"I don't think it was the casual break-in," said Maddox mildly.

"Well, obviously not," said D'Arcy. "Personal motive of some kind. Everything neat and clean. The wife?"

"You're just too cynical about people. I wonder." Maddox looked around the quiet, elegantly appointed room. There were books in a built-in shelf across one wall, but they looked unused: an appurtenance. The only picture in the room, if you could call it that, was a big framed coat of arms over the mantel. It displayed three scarlet griffins upright, and as a crest a mailed fist holding a sword. There was a Latin motto under it with an English translation under that: *What I take I hold.*

"Turn the lab loose on it," he said. He felt rather at a loss on this one. Another offbeat one.

D'Arcy went out to the squad to call the lab, and Maddox went back to the living room. Seen closer, it was a coldly sterile room full of stiff formal furniture; the high vaulted ceiling made it seem colder.

"Mrs. Mainwaring, can you tell me who Mr. Sanford is?"

"His lawyer," she said listlessly.

"But, ma'am, they ought to let you call Mr. Jim—he ought to know—" The maid appealed to Maddox. "The son—he ought to know about it—some burglar breaking in and shooting—"

"Would you like us to call your son, Mrs. Mainwaring?"

She had a handkerchief pressed to her lips. "Yes, thank you, maybe you'd better. His apartment—the number's in Charles' address book—"

CHAPTER 4

The son wasn't at home. The maid said he lived in an apartment, wasn't married. Baker, Franks and the newest lab technician, Garcia, were busy dusting the study, after getting the photographs. After they'd had a look at the wife's bedroom, the maid's, looked around the rest of the big house, looking primarily for the gun, Maddox had let her go to get dressed. He and D'Arcy had had a very thorough look at her bedroom; he had explained that they wouldn't need a legal warrant, in a homicide investigation, but she didn't register any protest. It was a big airy bedroom with its own bath, at the front of the house, and obviously she occupied it alone: no male clothing in the large adjoining closet, and the female clothes there were expensive but nothing garish. She had a little collection of expensive-looking jewelry. They looked through all the drawers, but didn't find anything suggestive, and no gun.

"Waste of time," said D'Arcy. "She's not a fool, if she shot him she wouldn't shove the gun away under her handkerchiefs, she'd know we'd look. It would make better sense to drop it there, make it look like suicide."

And of course the probable answer to that was that the gun had been removed because it might be traced to somebody. Or somebody thought it might be. Or somebody just wasn't thinking straight.

"You never know what a woman'll do," said Maddox.

They had talked to the maid while Mrs. Mainwaring was upstairs. The maid was divorced; she had gone to see her daughter on her night out, up in Altadena, and she'd gotten home about eleven o'clock. Of course she'd noticed the light on in the study when she drove in, but Mr. Mainwaring usually sat up till then, and her room was downstairs at the back, she wouldn't hear him go upstairs. She had gone to bed and hadn't heard a thing all night. "Do you think he was dead then, before Mrs. Mainwaring and I got home? My God, I never had such a shock in my life, walk in and find him dead—at first I thought a heart attack, and then I saw the blood—do you think it was a burglar?"

"We don't know," said D'Arcy. "Have you worked here long? Are they good people to work for?"

"Oh, sure," she said readily, "or I wouldn't have stayed ten years. They're quiet people, never entertain hardly at all, it's an easy place, just breakfast and dinner, and a regular cleaning service for all the heavy work. Mrs. Mainwaring'll be out with her friends or shopping most days, and he's at business all day, he owned a lot of property, shopping centers and office buildings and all like that."

"They get on all right together? Didn't quarrel?"

She didn't seem to have any old-family-retainer reticence. "Oh, sure," she said. "I never heard them have any fights, they're just quiet people like I said."

"They've just got the one son?"

"That's right. Mr. Jim. He just got out of college last year and went to work for Mr. Mainwaring's company. I never saw much of him, he'd be about twelve or thirteen when I came to work here, he was away at military school and then college, Stanford he went to." It hadn't entered her head that they were asking anything but random questions; she was still thinking about the burglar.

Now they were talking to the wife, who was keeping any emotions very much under control. She had given them her name, Avis Marcia Mainwaring, in a steady low voice. She sat on the long tapestry-covered couch in the enormous living room, opposite them, and answered questions with automatic courtesy. She was discreetly made up now, wearing a plain black sheath dress and black pumps, no jewelry except her wedding and engagement rings. She had a neat trim figure; she must have been a very beautiful young girl, and was still an extremely attractive woman at perhaps ten years younger than her husband.

"We understand you were out last evening, Mrs. Mainwaring," said Maddox.

"Yes, at a little dinner party at some friends' house. Charles hated what he called socializing, and everybody knew that—nobody expected him to go out much." She smiled faintly. "He didn't mind my going out, just so I didn't expect him to."

"Where were you?"

"Oh, at the Ellingers'—Tom and Evelyn Ellinger, in Beverly Hills. They're old friends. It was just a little dinner party, six of us, and we just sat around and talked after dinner. It was about eleven when I got home."

"Did you drive yourself?" asked D'Arcy.

Her mouth looked a little taut. "Well, actually I don't like to drive at night, one of the other guests picked me up and drove me home. Mr. Paxton, Mr. Joel Paxton, he's an old friend of ours."

"Did he come in with you?"

"Oh, no, it was late, he just dropped me off. I was tired, I went straight up to bed."

"You didn't look in on your husband in his study?—if he was there then? Did you notice if the light was on there?"

"I'm afraid I didn't," she said evenly. "I knew he was probably still up, he'd said he had some business letters to write, and I didn't disturb him." She held Maddox's eyes limpidly. For some unknown reason, thin dark unhandsome Maddox, who had just scraped into the force at five-nine, held some mysterious attraction for the females, and he realized that she had recognized it instantly, was playing on it, assuming that he would reciprocate. She gave him another little smile. "I very seldom went into the study, you see. It was—Charles' private place. He was a great reader, you know—only he didn't like any of the modern authors, just the classics." So Maddox had been wrong about the shelves of books. "He always said the old-fashioned authors never let you down."

"Had anybody ever let him down, Mrs. Mainwaring?"

"Oh, I didn't mean—it was just a figure of speech."

"Do you know anyone who had any reason to kill your husband? Had he had trouble with anyone lately?"

She shook her head, pressing a handkerchief to her lips. "There's nobody—no reason—I don't know what happened, or why. It was the most terrible shock when Amy woke me up and told me—how she'd found him— Why would anyone kill Charles? We thought first of a burglar—breaking in—but you could see there hadn't been any—any struggle—I just can't imagine what happened."

"Had he had any business trouble lately?"

"He hadn't mentioned anything, but he didn't talk much about business to me. I suppose they'd know at the office." She bent her neat blond head. "It just doesn't seem like anything that could happen— Charles getting killed. He was only fifty-seven. It's just—impossible. Fantastic."

"Do you know if he owned a gun?"

"I think he had one in his desk—in case of burglars—was—was that the one he was shot with? He wanted to show me how to use it once, but I'm afraid of guns, I wouldn't touch it."

"Was he at home when you left last night?"

"Oh, yes. Amy would be out, but he said he didn't want much for dinner—he'd met some man he was doing business with, and they'd had a late lunch. Amy just left out some cold cuts and cheese for sandwiches, and coffee on the stove. Mr. Paxton came about a quarter to six, and Charles let him in—he was drinking a whiskey and soda then, he usually had one before dinner—and I was all ready and we left right away." She put one of her pretty hands to her temple distractedly. "I'm sorry—I just can't tell you any more—I don't think I've really realized it yet, that he's dead—"

"We'll have to ask you to let us take your fingerprints, Mrs. Mainwaring—to compare with any others."

"Oh," she said. "I see." Clearly, she didn't. "All right, I don't mind. But I'd like to go up and rest now."

Baker came in to roll her prints, and they let her go.

"It's a nice smooth act, if it is an act," said D'Arcy. "But the way people like this live—the separate bedrooms, her going out without him—could be natural. For them."

Maddox said, "I'd like to know who he had lunch with. What business deals he'd been in lately. Evidently he didn't just live on the income, took an active part in the business. I wonder if he inherited the money, or made it, or just augmented it. Tomorrow we'll be asking questions at his office. Let's see how the lab's doing."

Franks and Baker had progressed into the dining room now; it would be a long job to cover this big place thoroughly. In the study Garcia was just finishing dusting the mantel. Once they'd gotten the photographs they had called the morgue, and the body was gone. "Well, there's that," said Garcia, and showed them a Colt .38. "In the top left-hand desk drawer. It hasn't been fired in a long time, and it's clean—no prints on it." It was fully loaded.

"He wasn't shot with anything as big as that," said Maddox.

"Something else a little interesting," said Garcia. "It was in the bottom shelf of the bookcase." He handed Maddox a long fat cardboard tube. Inside it, rolled up, was an elaborate and impressive-looking family tree, a genealogical record done in four colors looking long enough to date back to Adam and Eve.

"Shall I try to raise the son again?" asked D'Arcy.

"Might as well. We want to talk to him. And these people she was with last night. And the lawyer—" Maddox was staring at the coat of arms, rocking back and forth a little, heel to toe. "Come to think of it, D'Arcy, why was he writing the lawyer? Why not phone? He was an old-fashioned gent, though—no typewriter."

"Also," said D'Arcy, "no sign that he'd been writing business letters. Why the hell would he be, at home on Saturday night? He had an office, and I suppose a secretary. Typists."

"Yes," said Maddox, "that had occurred to me too. 'What I take I hold.' I get the impression that he was a very self-confident fellow, Mainwaring—everything well under control— Yes. Kind who might well have ridden a little roughshod over somebody, over business or something else. Might have gotten somebody's back up."

"And it might have been his wife's," said D'Arcy. "Why spin the tale about the business letters?"

"It could have been what he told her, you know. Just maybe, if she went her separate way, so did he. Did you come across any correspondence in the desk?" Maddox asked Garcia.

"Not much of anything—I didn't think he used it much. The two bottom drawers were empty, and just his address book and pen refills in the top drawer. It's all been dusted."

Maddox began to look through the address book, and D'Arcy picked up the phone.

Rodriguez had been feeling frustrated. He had tried those three addresses in Long Beach first, and drawn blank. C. Hinman was a luscious blonde about twenty; her name was Cynthia. The first Charles Hinman was a hulking hairy bus driver with a large family, all at home. The third address was a duplex, a neat stucco place on a quiet residential street in a middling good area of town. There was nobody home on either side, and no names on the mailboxes. He didn't know Long Beach, and had a little hunt for Lester's shoe store; it was on a secondary main drag. He spotted the sign as he drove past, parked and walked back; there'd be an emergency number posted on the door. But the store wasn't there anymore, only the sign: there was a CLOSED notice in the front window, and peering in he could see that the place was empty.

There was a chain drugstore on the corner; he talked to one of the clerks. Oh, that store went out of business about a month ago, she said. "It's a big chain, you know, but I guess business hadn't been so good and they closed this store or moved it some other place." He asked if she knew any of the people who had worked there. "Gee, no, how would I?" He described Hinman, but she just shook her head.

The only other place open on the block was a brightly painted chain coffee shop, and there he had better luck. The toothy brunette at the cash register said oh, that place, the men worked there used to come in for lunch. "We're the only restaurant for six blocks around." There were three of them, two young fellows and an older man. She listened to the description and nodded. "That's the older one, I never heard his name—you a private eye of some kind?"

"Looking for a witness," said Rodriguez. "You wouldn't know where he lived?"

"My goodness, no, he was just a customer."

And of course Hinman might not be living immediately in town, just somewhere closer than he had been in Hollywood. Rodriguez had a look, at the pay phone, at the adjacent phone book to that covering the southern beach cities, and found a C. M. Hinman listed in La Mirada. He drove up there. It was a new apartment house, and nobody was home at the apartment, but the woman next door told him that the Hinmans were just a young couple, only married six months.

He stopped and had lunch, and went back to the duplex in Long Beach. This time he got a response at one door, an elderly man who said, "Oh, Mr. Hinman lived on the other side. My name's Fenton, I own this place. . . . No, I'm sorry, I don't know where he moved. He left last Monday." Rodriguez repeated the description and he nodded. "Yes, that's Hinman. A very nice fellow—quiet tenant. He rented the place for about two and a half years. I haven't advertised it yet because I want to get it painted. They moved in about a year ago last May—"

"They?"

"Well, his wife was alive then. Why are you asking about him, anyway?"

"We think he witnessed an accident, might have to testify about it. He was married?"

"Why, yes. Nice woman, sort of shy. It was a terrible blow to him when she was killed—she'd only be in her forties, I suppose—but accidents can happen to anybody. She was back east visiting her sister when she got killed, he went back for the funeral."

"When was that?"

"Oh, last year, April or May. He said he was originally from Glassboro, New Jersey, but I seem to recall it was some place else she got killed—Iowa or Indiana. Then, when the store where he worked was getting closed, they transferred him way up to the valley somewhere, so naturally he had to move."

"Do you remember where he was transferred?"

"Glendale—or was it Glendora? I couldn't say."

The local post office had no record of a forwarding address.

Rodriguez headed back for Hollywood, annoyed. He didn't know where the headquarters office of that shoe chain was—find out tomorrow? And, or, look at the stores in those two towns. At least, when the man had moved only last Monday, they should catch up to him on the next try. But he wondered about the wife. Of course they had talked to only one other fellow who had known him—that clerk—and Hinman might be the kind who didn't talk about his family. He could have had the wife all along. Which made it unlikelier that he had had anything to do with the bodies.

Mrs. Siegel came into the station about three o'clock, and just as they'd expected promptly identified the composite sketch. "That's him —the one who shot Mr. Pike—I'll never forget that face. You want him for something already?" She signed a statement, and Feinman was just filing it when Maddox and D'Arcy came in and gave him a rundown on the new homicide.

"Well, I may have collected a little new business for us too," said Feinman. "Charles Dickens." He told them about that. "And I'll be damned if it isn't really his name, he had the I.D. to prove it. He's a cook at a cafeteria across town, he's got no pedigree at all, and he kept saying he did too murder that woman. Eighteen years ago. He only knew her first name, he picked her up in a bar on Third, and when they got outside in the parking lot something came over him and he picked up a brick and hit her on the head. He didn't rob her, he didn't know why he killed her. And he's hit a lot of other women on the head too, since then, only he doesn't think he killed any of them. He keeps getting this funny impulse to hit women over the head, and he thinks maybe there's something wrong with him. I ask you."

D'Arcy laughed. "But, my God," said Feinman, "eighteen years— just to find out if there was such a homicide we'd have to look back for the record of the inquest, and it'd be on microfilm in the old records at the courthouse—"

"What did you tell him?" asked Maddox.

"I told him to go home and we'd get in touch if we wanted him. I've got his address."

"Well, maybe we'd better follow it up. If he's honest, there may damn well be something wrong with him, and we don't want him committing another homicide, Joe. I suppose he'd get sent for a psychiatric examination, at least. I want to call home, find out how Sue is." He picked up the phone.

"And another church got vandalized," said Feinman.

"Hell," said D'Arcy. "I'll see if I can get Jim Mainwaring again."

Maddox had just finished talking to Sue, who was feeling better, when Rodriguez came in and passed on what he'd found out about Hinman.

"I think the main plant of that chain is back east somewhere, but there ought to be a regional office out here, you'd think. They could tell us definitely where Hinman was transferred. Quicker to have a look at the stores in Glendale and Glendora, of course."

"They seem to transfer their personnel around a lot," said D'Arcy.

"Some of these big chains do—don't give a damn about personal convenience. But damn it," said Rodriguez, "he was at that house at the relevant time, if the doctors know what they're talking about at all —and I'd like to find him."

Just then Dowling came in towing one of the possibles from the sex-offender list, and Feinman went to sit in on the questioning.

And this time D'Arcy found Jim Mainwaring at home, and he and Maddox went out again.

Just after Maddox and D'Arcy had left, Bill Nolan brought another possible in and said to Rodriguez, "This one could be hot. On several counts."

Rodriguez heard about him and agreed. His name was Enrico Morales, and he didn't have a very nice record—child molestation, narco use, enticement of minors for immoral purposes, attempted assault, rape of minor. He had served some time in the joint. He was thirty now, and he wasn't a prepossessing sight. He was heavy-shouldered and bulky, unshaven and dirty, with long greasy hair, a straggling mustache, furtive eyes and a sullen mouth. He was very much a possible for Bobby Kelsey.

He called them all the expectable names and snarled and evaded, but they kept pounding at him and got a few facts established, and he started to look even better. From their point of view.

He admitted that he'd been along Hollywood Boulevard last Tuesday afternoon. He had a couple of pals who worked at a store along there. Translation, one of the porn bookshops. He didn't wear a watch, he couldn't say what time he left there, he didn't remember where he'd gone next or when he got home, he didn't know nothing about no kid, he hadn't done nothing to no kid. But he was living with his brother in an apartment on Leland Way, and that was significantly close to where Bobby Kelsey had been found. He had an old heap of a car. The brother worked the swing shift at an assembly plant. Morales would have had the time and a place to do what was done to Bobby Kelsey.

But it was up in the air. Rodriguez, gauging the type, didn't think Morales would break very easy or quick. They went on at him, patiently and relentlessly, until five-thirty, and then told him he could go.

"God, these types," said Nolan. His deceptively youthful face wore a look of disgust. They went back to the big office, out of the cramped interrogation room with its inadequate chairs. Rodriguez offered him a cigarette. "Someday you'll remember I don't smoke."

"Sorry." Rodriguez lit one. Nolan might be young to make rank, and look as if he might be a nance, but he would shape into a good detective; there was more to him than showed on the surface.

"He's about the likeliest we've come across, I'd say. What do you think?"

"He might be. Get a search warrant for that apartment," said Rodriguez lazily, leaning back. "The ones like that don't realize what scientific evidence can be turned up. Fibers from the boy's clothes, blood of his type, there might be enough to pin down the charge. It's worth a try."

"That was in my mind." Nolan nodded. "The lab can work some miracles."

"But we can't depend on them," said Rodriguez. "You can go apply for the warrant. It ought to be in tomorrow."

"Sure."

"And I am going home. I've had a long day."

Jim Mainwaring looked like a young carbon copy of Charles Mainwaring. He was tall, with wide shoulders and lean hips; he had the same big, arrogant high-bridged nose and strong jaw, and a thick crest of auburn-brown hair. He looked about twenty-three, but even at that age he was already a definite personality.

The apartment was in West Hollywood, and it would rent for more than the average young man on his first job could afford, but Mainwaring had probably given him a hefty allowance or a very generous salary. It wasn't a big place, or fancily furnished, but it was a solidly good address, the living room more spacious than most. The furniture was Danish modern, and as they came in they noticed an easel set up in front of the big picture window, with a stretched canvas propped on it.

"You paint for a hobby, Mr. Mainwaring?" asked Maddox, to start the ball rolling.

Instead, it seemed to annoy him. He said shortly, "That's right." He was casually dressed in sports clothes in brown tones; not the conventionally handsome young man, but maybe one to reckon with. "Sit down. You might tell me your names again, I didn't catch—" He ran a hand through his hair. "God," he said, "I can't get over this, about Father. You gave me one hell of a shock when you called—I can't believe it. I don't know who'd want to murder Father. It doesn't seem possible—he's dead."

"Everybody always on good terms with him?" asked Maddox. "Including you?"

"Yes," said Mainwaring. "Certainly. Oh, he could be a bit of a tyrant in some ways, he was used to having his own way mostly, but that was Father. I—can't imagine him dead, you know," and on that he sounded young. "He was always—so alive. Positive. So much—well, in control. You said"—he got up and went over to look out the window —"you haven't found out anything about it. Who might have done it."

"We'll be looking around and asking questions. We'll hope to find out."

"Yes." He still had his back turned. He was silent, and then went on in a low voice, "Oh, he could be—difficult. Anybody'll tell you that. He—thought he always knew best. But under all that—he was a terribly proud man. Proud of his—his integrity. I—" He fell silent again for a long minute. "I suppose you noticed that coat of arms in his study. The Mainwaring coat of arms. He was very hot on family and genealogy—the old blood-will-tell bit, you know—there's a family tree somewhere. The first Mainwarings here came over slightly ahead of the Mayflower, I gather, and in England they go back to around the First Crusade. Always seemed a damn-fool sort of thing to boast about, to me, but it meant a lot to him. A lot."

"I see," said Maddox. "If you don't mind answering a few questions—"

"No. Sorry, I didn't mean to—it's just, I can't adjust to his—being dead. Bang. No warning."

"You work in the family company, we've heard."

"That's right. Only not family. I'm just the latest slave in the accounting department. Look, can we cut this short right now? I ought to go and see my mother—"

"We understand that," said D'Arcy, "but we'd like a few answers to go on with. Had there been any trouble there lately, did your father have any run-ins with employees or business associates?"

"I don't know, I don't think so. I didn't see much of him at the office, we've got two floors in the building and his office is above ours. If he wanted any records or accounts, he'd have them sent up. I don't know of any new deals under way or coming up—that there might have been trouble over—the only thing in the works is that shopping complex, and that's all arranged, the company bought the land last year. If there was anything like that, Mr. Gower would know—he's vice president—or Father's secretary, Rosalie Dutton. Mr. Schultz hasn't said anything—he's the chief accountant. Hell, if there'd been anything like that, you know the grapevine in an office, it'd have gotten around." He shook his head. "I just can't give you any idea what's behind it. Who might have done it."

"Do you own a gun, Mr. Mainwaring?"

He swung around, startled. "Me? A gun? My God, no—do you think *I* killed him?"

"Did you have a reason to?" asked Maddox.

He laughed harshly. "No," he said. "And no, I don't have a gun. I'm not interested in guns. And for the record, I didn't kill him."

"Where were you last evening, here?"

"No. I was out. I had dinner at a restaurant—an Italian place in Beverly Hills—with a friend of mine, and then I went to a movie."

"Alone? Who was the friend?"

"Rick Hyatt. He's a reporter for the *Herald*. He had some work to do after dinner."

"And what was the movie?"

"That theater in Hollywood that shows foreign films. They were showing a French film about Gauguin. My French isn't all that good, but it—passed the time. I got home about eleven."

"And where were you this morning?"

"Walking on the beach at Malibu. I like the beach. Look, I really had better go—"

"Yes, that's all right. We'll want to talk to you again later."

"God, I hope you find out about it. How it happened. It just doesn't seem possible he's gone."

In D'Arcy's Dodge on the street, Maddox asked, "Anything strike you?"

"I may just be wool-gathering. He's a strong personality, and we can gather that Mainwaring was too."

"In spades. Strong personalities frequently clash. But Mainwaring Senior controlled the money. The little thing that struck me," said Maddox, "may mean even less. Terminology."

"Which?"

"Father," said Maddox thoughtfully. "Well, we've heard that he was an old-fashioned man. That much? A little bit formal for everyday give and take in the family. There's also the military school."

For once D'Arcy caught his thought. "He wouldn't have lived at home much. But, Ivor—these people—with this much money—they don't use the same standards."

"That's probably very true." And it had finally started to rain again, and it was a quarter to six. D'Arcy started the engine. "I wonder just how long the lab will keep us waiting for a report. They always take their own sweet time. Did anybody remember to remind the morgue to send that slug over?"

"The doctors know the routine," said D'Arcy.

Sue met him at the back door and said she was feeling perfectly all right again, it had just been a little digestive upset. "Everybody I ever knew who's had a baby says they never felt better, all the time. And, Ivor, would you settle for Philip?"

"No. I won't be particular about a girl, unless you pick something outlandish, but a boy's going to be John."

"But for heaven's sake, there's nothing fancy or—or peculiar about David or Daniel or Richard or Jonathan or Alan—"

"I'm just being a purist." Maddox went to kiss Margaret's cheek.

"But it's so ordinary," said Sue. "It's not as if I wanted to saddle him with, well, something like your middle name—"

"God in heaven forbid," said Maddox. "And speaking of names, I think D'Arcy's feeling more cheerful the last day or so. I'll bet he broke up with the latest girl, so he's due to fall for a new one anytime. It's a pity he can't find some nice firm female who'd marry him out of hand and give him a good home."

Margaret was taking a roast out of the oven. "That's the poor fellow who's shy about his first name. I never heard what it was." Maddox told her, and she burst out laughing. "We'd better agree on John, Sue. The worst anybody can do with it is Johnny, and it wouldn't matter whether he's homely or handsome."

"Which is a thought only a grandmother would have," said Maddox. "But leaving me out of it, how could your beautiful daughter produce a homely offspring?"

"Flattery gets you nowhere," said Sue. "Sometimes you can be very tiresome, darling."

The night watch left them two new heists on Monday morning. Neither one seemed to have been pulled by the blond bunglers; both were slick pro jobs, a pharmacy and a liquor store. The first heister had worn a ski mask, so there'd be nothing more to get there; the second one was described by the liquor-store clerk as a young Latin type, with a mustache and sideburns. He had said he might recognize a picture, so somebody would have to stay on to take him downtown. It was D'Arcy's day off.

Rodriguez, who seemed hypnotized by the urgency of locating Hinman, set off for Glendora before he could get deflected onto anything else. There were still the sex offenders to hunt, and Maddox wanted to talk to the people at Mainwaring's office. But he and Feinman were still in, if just ready to leave, when two autopsy reports came up: on the little girl, Jean Fisher, and Esther Cook. There wasn't much in either of them. They had both died of skull fractures, and the Fisher girl had various broken bones and contusions. She'd been struck by something bigger than a little sports job. The doctor had sent her clothes to the lab. With what they could do in the way of analysis and photography, a lead might possibly turn up from that. Maddox passed the reports on to Feinman and stood up and stretched, reaching for his coat. It had gone on raining all night and it was still raining, a steady thin drizzle.

That search warrant was in for the Morales apartment; he hoped somebody at the lab would find time to execute it today. Yes, and sometime they ought to put in a request at the courthouse downtown to check on a possible inquest record, that eighteen-year-old homicide; and he knew the answer they'd get, an invitation to come down and look for themselves, nobody there had the time. He wondered if they'd get some kind of kickback from NCIC on that description, and if so when. Of course they had a lot of computers back there.

Morales sounded like a fairly hot suspect, but unless they could get some scientific evidence they'd never pin it on him. And a hotter suspect might show.

Mainwaring. They didn't often get the complex mysteries; if somebody had had a motive to take him off, it would show up. Check on the wife's evening out, talk to people who knew them. If either of them had been two-timing, that would show too.

The phone rang on his desk. He swore, but reached for it automatically. "Sergeant Maddox, Hollywood."

"Say, this is Dave Brubeck, I got a pawnshop on Vine. I just been looking over the latest hot list you sent out, and there's this bicycle— green and white three-speed Schwinn—we got one like that. My clerk took it in last Friday."

"What?" said Maddox. It had just been a gesture to put that bicycle on the hot list. Damnation, he thought, they'd have to round up Kelsey, see if he could identify it positively. There hadn't been any distinguishing marks on Bobby Kelsey's bike—there'd be a thousand like it all over town—and he'd always thought the odds were that some kid had come across that bike, where the Kelsey boy was grabbed off it, and just quietly appropriated it. Or some adult.

"You there?" asked Brubeck.

"Yes, yes. Somebody'll be down to look at it. I suppose whoever brought it in signed a release?"

"Yeah, I got it right here. Frank said it was a black guy. See if I can make it out—he didn't write too clear—it's Snell. Henry Snell. I can't read the address at all."

"All right, somebody'll be down." Maddox replaced the phone and sat staring into space, unseeingly. "Snell. Now where the hell have I heard that just recently? Snell. I can't connect it up with—wait a minute, don't distract me, Joe, it was something to do with—" And thirty seconds later he leaped up and shouted, "*Snell!* By God—but for Christ's sake, what a goddamned stupid thing—if that's the answer—"

The thin little black woman looked up at them nervously, in the doorway of that court unit on Harvard. "You want Henry?" she said. "He took off somewhere yesterday, I don't know where." She was frightened. "He's done something else bad again, the cops looking for him, hasn't he? I don't know what's wrong with him, he can't stay outta trouble." She shook her head. "He been talking some about going to live with this buddy of his in Santa Monica, but like I told him, he'd have to make it all right with Mr. Kershaw. That's his parole officer. Seems like a nice man."

Maddox asked very gently, "Your son's on parole?"

"Yes, sir, he's on parole from the penitentiary up north. They said he did something awful to a little girl, that was just the last time he got in trouble."

Martin Kershaw blew into the station like a typhoon thirty minutes after Maddox had called Welfare and Rehab downtown. He was raving mad, and for the first five minutes they just listened to a lot of colorful expletives. Sue and Daisy came to find out what was going on as he started to calm down just a little. He was a smallish man about thirty-five, with a thatch of bright-red hair.

"I said they were crazy—I told everybody at the office, we all knew it was crazy—oh, Christ, that goddamned parole board! It's the goddamned parole board they ought to stash in the joint, for Christ's sweet sake! He did less than three years this last time, dear God, for raping and killing a five-year-old, there was a plea bargain and they called it murder two and gave him ten to twenty, and he's out in twenty-six months—Christ, all the times they've let him out—the goddamn fool head doctors, now he's cured—you don't cure one like that—Jesus Christ, you won't believe the record—"

Snell's record went back to age eighteen; what he might have done as a juvenile they didn't know, the rules so protective of minors didn't let the law keep records on them. He was thirty-two now, and the record said child molestation, enticement of minors, assault, assault with intent to rape, and it said homicide. He had attacked and killed a ten-year-old boy ten years ago, the charge reduced to second degree, he had gotten a five-to-fifteen and been paroled after three years. Altogether he had attacked and injured seven children—that the authorities knew about—and had killed two of them. Altogether, he had served eight years and nine months in minimum security prisons. This last time he had been out on parole for four months.

"Christ in heaven!" said Kershaw savagely. "The goddamn parole board are the criminals—I've seen some cases to make me sick, but this is the bloody end—I don't give a good goddamn if it costs me the job, I'm going to spread this all over every newspaper with the guts to print it! I don't suppose the poor goddamn taxpayers can stop this comic-book governor from appointing the softheaded bleeding hearts to the bench, but we can goddamn well rub their noses in it and tell them how decent people feel—by Christ—"

They had an A.P.B. out on him then; he was driving an old Ford. His mother had told them the name of the buddy in Santa Monica, and they'd asked that force to go and look.

In the end, at eleven-thirty, it was just that simple. Snell was there at his buddy's at a room on Second Street, and the Santa Monica boys ferried him up.

He scowled at them all standing around him where he sat in the chair beside Maddox's desk. He was a big man, very black, flabby and soft, but three times the size of thirteen-year-old Bobby Kelsey. He was mad at them for picking him up, and he wasn't much of a brain, but he understood that they had some kind of proof on him.

"So all right, that kid," he said reluctantly, sullenly. "I seen him—gettin' the money for the newspaper, he was talkin' to that Mis' Ostermeyer. When he come ridin' past, I opened the door and says maybe I like to buy his paper, he come right over." Bobby the regular little businessman. "Ma was at her job at the restaurant."

They asked him questions, but not for long. "I put the bike in the garage, Ma never goes there, she don't drive. I thought I might get a few bucks for it. Oh, I threw away that little book he had. Look—look, see, I never meant to hurt the kid bad—look, you tell my ma, get that same lawyer I had last time—he's a smart talker, he can tell the judge all about it, how I never mean to hurt anybody so I only go back in the joint awhile—"

By two o'clock it was all wrapped up, the paperwork done, Snell in the old Wilcox Street jail, and Maddox and Feinman were driving down Sunset to talk to the people in Mainwaring's office.

"But I think," said Maddox, "it'd be the only kind thing to do, Joe, to see Roy Kelsey personally and tell him about Henry Snell. Before he sees the papers."

CHAPTER 5

Rodriguez had tried Glendale first, but the Lester's store there didn't know anything about Hinman, so he'd driven over to Glendora. At the Lester's store there, in a new and glittering shopping center, he was talking to a handsome dark young fellow, Art Romero.

"It was a hell of a lucky break for me, you can see that. I never expected to get promotion so soon—I've only worked for them three years, but of course I was on the spot, and know the business. This Hinman—I never saw the man—he was supposed to take over as manager here, when the new store opened a couple of weeks ago. Then the superintendent of the regional office contacted me—it's a national chain, I suppose you know—I was at the store in Pomona, I was getting transferred over here, and he said Hinman had quit and as long as I was going to be here anyway he'd try me out as manager. A damned lucky break."

"Hinman resigned from his job?" said Rodriguez blankly. "Why?"

Romero shrugged widely. "How do I know?"

"Well, where can I find this superintendent? What's his name?"

"McGuire. It's downtown L.A., Olive Street."

Rodriguez looked up the address. When he got there, it was a rather bare, shabby old office in an old building. Lester's was a cut-rate chain advertising low prices, and evidently didn't believe in wasting money on fancy surroundings. McGuire was a middle-aged man, coolly efficient, all the facts in his mind without looking up records. He swallowed the witness story whole, and shrugged, and said, "Well, I'm afraid we can't help you much. I thought it was a little strange, Hinman was such a steady reliable man. He had a very good record with us. And a man of his age wouldn't find it easy to change jobs."

"Did he give any reason for quitting? Did he phone you, or what?"

"I had a letter." McGuire, who was small and spare and brisk, hopped up and went to the door. There was a minute front office where a buck-toothed dark girl presided over a typewriter and telephone. "Doris, look up that letter from Hinman. Some time last week." He came back and sat down again. "He'd been working for us for nearly thirty years—"

"That long?"

"Around there. He'd worked at a good many of our stores. It's a national chain, as you know. He was sent out here from somewhere in Ohio, I think, and he'd been transferred around here. Some employees don't like to be asked to move from store to store, and we try not to make it mandatory. But Hinman never seemed to mind." The girl came in with the letter. "Oh, thanks, Doris. There you are, you see what he says." He handed the letter over. It was brief, neatly written by hand in a plain script curiously without character, on a sheet of plain paper, headed with the address of the duplex in Long Beach. "'Dear Mr. McGuire, I am very sorry to inconvenience you at short notice, but would like to offer my resignation. Since losing my dear wife, my health has been very uncertain and I do not feel that I could go on giving satisfaction. I am thinking of returning to my original home in the east, or somewhere nearby where I lived as a young man. I have enjoyed working for the firm all these years. Yours Truly, Charles Hinman.'"

"Short notice all right," said Rodriguez. "He's about fifty-five, isn't he? Too young to retire—and he wouldn't find it easy to change jobs these days."

"We'd give him a very good recommendation, of course, if he applied somewhere."

"He told his recent landlord he hailed originally from Glassboro, New Jersey."

"Oh, I couldn't say—I didn't know him, only by his record with us. The headquarters office in New York would have the complete records of wherever he'd worked for the company. He was moved to California, as far as I recall, around ten years ago. I think from Ohio. He'd been at a number of our stores here—Hawthorne, Pasadena, Hollywood, Manhattan Beach, Thousand Oaks. But there's another thing, Mr. Rodriguez—he didn't give us any address to send the salary we still owe him. It seems—uncharacteristic. But of course, if he hadn't actually made up his mind where he was going—" McGuire shrugged. "We may hear from him when he gets settled somewhere."

"If you do," said Rodriguez, "let us know, will you? We'd really like to talk to him."

"Surely, I'd be glad to."

Rodriguez got back to the station just in time to walk into all the excitement on Henry Snell.

John Gower said to Maddox and Feinman, "It's been a great shock. Charles' wife called me last night. I simply couldn't believe it, Charles murdered—the crime rate these days—but you say it wasn't the common thief breaking in— It's hard to believe there could be any personal motive." He shook his head at them gravely. He was probably about the same age as Mainwaring, a little pompous, a little too aware of his own importance. The offices of the Mainwaring Management and Investment Company, in a high-rise building out on Sunset, were impressive and expensive. Mainwaring's and Gower's offices were on the eighth floor, with a view over the city. Gower was tall and thin, with a gray mustache and horn-rimmed glasses, the stereotyped executive.

"There wasn't anything worrying him about the business?" asked Maddox. "Any difficulty or trouble here?"

"Certainly not—no, of course not."

"We understand he saw someone about some business on Saturday, would you know—"

Gower was turning a pipe around and around in his hands. "Oh, yes, we both met Hersheimer on Saturday, we were thinking of buying a piece of property in Chatsworth, we met him there to look at it, but he's asking too much. We took him to lunch and dickered around most of the afternoon, but didn't come to any agreement. Charles left to go home about a quarter to four. I can't understand this—he was just as usual, didn't seem worried about anything, he never said a word about any personal trouble—"

"Would he have?" asked Feinman.

Gower coughed, fiddled with the pipe, gave them a sideways glance. "Well, er, there is that—quite true. He was a very self-contained man. I suppose I knew him well in a business sense, but I don't know that he would have, er, confided in me about any personal worry"—he looked speculatively curious—"oh, say over his wife or something like that."

"You didn't see much of each other socially?" asked Maddox.

"Well, no, I can't say that we did. I lost my wife a few years ago, I don't entertain widely, and Charles wasn't a man to gad around socially, he didn't care for parties or the theater. We knew some of the same people, naturally, but no, we didn't, er, see much of each other outside of business. If he'd been worried about some financial matter, something to do with the firm, I'd have known about it, but there wasn't anything like that. Definitely. The company's never been in better shape."

They didn't get much from Gower. By what they did get, he didn't have much to give them. For all Gower had been an officer in the firm for years, he and Mainwaring hadn't been close friends. He could tell them about the company. The Mainwaring fortune was old money; his grandfather had brought it west from New England in the 1880s and been shrewd and lucky in land investments in the growth of the new state.

The secretary, Mrs. Dutton, hadn't anything to offer either; she was shocked and upset. No glamor girl, she was a plain middle-aged woman looking efficient and sensible.

On the way down to the accounting department on the seventh floor, Maddox said, "If he had a girl friend on the side nobody here knew about it. He was just the big businessman of rigid principle at the office, and all business, no light touches—you get the same impression, Joe?"

"That's about it. He sounds like a pretty cold fish to me, not letting anybody get very close to him. I wonder if he was the same way with the family."

"They're both acting all correct and conventional too. If there was any jealousy or hate or—mmh, any secrets floating around, they're not letting it show."

The accounting department occupied a good deal more space than the executive offices on the floor above. In a long, wide, open office, semiprivacy was achieved by partitions shutting off little cubicles for each employee; each cubicle had a desk, files, a phone. At the far end of the room was a door labeled PERSONNEL. The cubicle of the chief accountant, Bernard Schultz, faced that. There'd be a lot of accounts and records to keep in this kind of business: this big a business.

Schultz was a little thin gray man, probably at least sixty, with a tight mouth and shrewd gray eyes. They didn't see Jim Mainwaring anywhere around, and one of the cubicles was unoccupied.

"It's a terrible thing," said Schultz quietly, conventionally. "It just seems incredible, Mr. Mainwaring getting murdered. You haven't found out who did it yet?"

"We'll be investigating. I see young Mr. Mainwaring isn't here today. That's understandable."

"Yes," said Schultz.

"I suppose," said Feinman heartily, "he'll step into his father's place now—he's pretty young and inexperienced for so much responsibility, isn't he?"

"I really don't know," said Schultz expressionlessly. "Mr. Mainwaring was a very astute man, he'd probably arranged for all possible contingencies. He'll be missed in the firm, but of course Mr. Gower is very competent." He went on answering questions unenthusiastically. Mr. Mainwaring had seemed his usual self on Friday. Schultz wouldn't, of course, have known anything about any personal worries, or trouble. Yes, young Mr. Mainwaring was well liked in the office, and shaping up well at his job.

The door marked PERSONNEL opened and a woman came out, and up to Schultz's desk. She was a rather scraggly middle-aged woman with suspiciously dark brown hair. The company didn't seem to go in for glamorous girl Fridays. "Oh, Mr. Schultz, Mr. Hauser wants to see you—oh, excuse me, I didn't know you were busy."

"Quite all right, Mrs. French. What is it?"

"About that letter of recommendation for Mancini. He wants to know if you'll authorize it."

"All right, I'll be there in a few minutes." She looked a little curiously at Maddox and Feinman and went back to the other office. The office would be buzzing with curiosity and speculation about the murder, but on the surface nobody would suspect it.

They didn't get anything remotely suggestive there at all, except by inference more evidence on the murdered man's character. And it was now after five o'clock.

They couldn't say it had been an unproductive day. They had gotten Snell, and this time—they hoped—he'd go up for Murder One.

The night watch left them another heist on Tuesday morning, and there were no possible leads on it at all, no description, even vague; it had been an all-night pharmacy on Vermont, and the heister had cleaned out all the drugs as well as about a hundred bucks from the register. There was nowhere to go on that, except to haul in the men from Records to question

They kicked the Mainwaring thing around, but they didn't really have enough yet to reach any conclusions. "I want to see the people his wife was with that night," said Maddox. "What's the name—Ellinger, Beverly Hills. And the man who chauffeured her—Paxton. I looked him up—he's a lawyer, Paxton, Dexter and Lynch, a classy address on Elevado Avenue. And damn it, I ought to get hold of Mainwaring's lawyer, this Sanford—I looked him up too, he evidently practices alone, his office is on Sunset, home address Chatham Drive. I don't suppose we could decently call anybody in Beverly Hills until nine o'clock at least, and the lawyer ought to be in his office by then."

But when, on the stroke of nine, he called the Ellinger house, a voice identifying itself as the maid informed him that Mrs. Ellinger was out, she wouldn't be back until late, and Mr. Ellinger was out of town looking at some horses. "Horses?" said Maddox blankly.

"Yes, sir, he owns a lot of racehorses. He said he might be back tomorrow. Can I take a message, sir?"

Frustrated, Maddox called Sanford's office. A secretary tried to get rid of him, but he was firm with her, kept reminding her who he was, and finally Sanford came on. "Did you say sergeant? Sergeant who? Oh, yes." He sounded friendly enough, if slightly harried. "Well, look, Sergeant, Betty wasn't upstaging you, I really am busy as hell, up to my neck in this damned libel suit. I know you'll want to talk to me—this is the damndest thing about Mainwaring getting murdered, Gower called me yesterday and then Mainwaring's wife—I never had a client murdered before, and I don't know a damned thing about it, I didn't know Mainwaring very well personally, even if I had been his lawyer, and the company's, for about twelve years. But you'll want to know about his affairs in general, his will. The wife wants me to arrange the funeral—"

"Well, you understand there has to be an autopsy. We can let you know when the body will be released."

"Yes, I understand that. I have to be in court all day, and probably tomorrow too, I'll be lucky if the bench adjourns by five, and I've got a conference set up with my client later on. Suppose we try to make it Thursday—I think the case ought to go to the jury by afternoon, but at least I'll be free Thursday evening."

"Well, if that's the best you can do, sir—"

"I haven't got ten minutes till then." Sanford rang off briskly.

Maddox was annoyed. "There's Paxton—and we'd better see that Hyatt, Jim Mainwaring's pal. Said to be on the *Herald*."

"If he's a pal, he wouldn't pass on any family secrets," said Feinman. "And speaking of the media, did any of you see the *Times?*" Kershaw had carried out his threat with a vengeance. There was an interview with him on the front page this morning; and even the liberal *Times,* sensing the general temper of *hoi polloi,* had a grave and stern editorial about the dangers of softness on criminals and, more to the point, a complete breakdown of Snell's record. Over the next few weeks, probably, there would be a spate of letters to the editor. And tonight the *Herald* would probably carry an even stronger editorial; that was the more conservative sheet.

"We'll hope to get something concrete from the lab report," said Maddox, "if they ever send us one." His phone rang. "Oh, for God's sake, not a new call." He picked it up. "Sergeant Maddox."

"And a good morning to you," said a genial bass voice. "Sergeant Gearhart here, down at the lab, headquarters. We just sent a report up to you by messenger, and I think you'll find it interesting. It's always gratifying to have a difficult job turn out the way you hoped."

"A report on what?"

"This body your boys found buried somewhere up on your beat. The coroner's office said to report back to you. They sent over a few rags of clothes they got off it, and I've been having a look the best way I could. There wasn't much to look at. What was once a dress, nylon knit of some kind, and the remnants of a pair of shoes. The label inside one of those came up a little bit under the microscope, and I'm pretty sure it says Leeds—"

"Oh, hell," said Maddox. "Another low-priced chain."

"Yes, but wait for it. There was something else. The body was apparently on its back, and the back and upper part of the dress were still hanging together. It probably wouldn't have occurred to me, but my wife sews a lot, makes most of the family's clothes, and somebody gave her these little personalized labels to sew in. Says *fashioned by,* and her name. And when I took a close look at the neck of that dress, there was this little tag just showing, and I guessed what it might be. I really gave it the works, tried four or five ways, and I finally brought it up—mostly—under ultraviolet. You ought to get the report any minute."

"You brought up a name?" Maddox was incredulous.

"That's just what. Partly. I think it could give you a place to go, anyway."

Maddox thanked him. "Our scientific miracle men. What would we do without you?"

Gearhart chuckled. "I tell you, Maddox, it's an easier job than yours. At least we get to sit down most of the time. And stay out of the rain."

Five minutes later the messenger delivered the report. They didn't bother to read the typed form, shared out the glossy eight-by-ten photographs. "By God," said Rodriguez reverently, "what they can do with their trick cameras!"

Two of them were sharper than the others. They were greatly magnified shots of a little scrap of fabric, originally light-colored but spotted with dark stains. Across the scrap were script letters in a darker color, chain-stitched. Not all of them were legible, a dark stain ran across the middle, but they could make out the letters FASH—Y—RO—PARFI.

"Oh, very nice," said Feinman. "Very pretty. Unless, of course, it's the label of some specialty shop in Beverly Hills. I take it this would be the body the doctors said was buried latest."

"Two to three years," said Maddox. "A place to go and ask questions, at least. We seem to be stymied on Mainwaring—and maybe we'd better wait to see the lab report before we go prodding at these people, anyway. I'll go down to see if there's any record on this—"

"And I'll go with you," said Rodriguez. "If there's any chance of identifying one of those bodies—¡Adelante!"

They didn't have to discuss where to go. At Parker Center, L.A.P.D. headquarters downtown, they rode up to the Missing Persons Bureau and explained their mission to a Sergeant Hammer. He looked at the photographs interestedly. "The things the lab can do. You said, back as far as three years, maybe?"

"Well, give it leeway—the doctors couldn't be sure."

Hammer said, "Our current files never are all that current, because sometimes people stay missing a long time. Most of them, of course, have gone missing deliberately—but not always. Let's have a look." They had everything cross-filed by names and dates, and there were a lot of files to look at, but of course they had a couple of clues. Within ten minutes they were looking at a folder on Mrs. Rose Parfitt, reported missing on a date of nearly forty months ago. She was described as a widow, aged forty-one, five-five, a hundred and forty pounds, brown hair and blue eyes. Her address was on Sierra Bonita in Hollywood. She had a job at a dress shop on Santa Monica Boulevard. She had been reported missing by her sister, Mrs. Roberta Larson, and her address was given as Virgil Avenue. Parfitt was reported to be a respectable woman who went to church, didn't drink or smoke, never went out alone at night.

Rodriguez demanded a phone book. "And there she still is," he said pleasedly, "the same address on Virgil. Talk about lucky breaks!"

"On chance in a million, all right," said Hammer. "I wonder how the hell the woman ended up murdered. But in the jungle, the wild ones anywhere."

Being halfway there, Maddox and Rodriguez went to find the Virgil Avenue address. It was a solid old red-brick apartment building, and

Mrs. Roberta Larson lived on the second floor. Maddox pushed the bell and presently a woman opened the door. She was about fifty, amply made and gray-haired, with a placid round face. She stared at the badges. "What do you want?" she asked.

"It's about your sister," said Maddox. "Your sister Rose."

Her eyes widened on him. "Have you found her—after all this time?"

"We don't know, Mrs. Larson," said Rodriguez, "but we think so. We'd like you to look at something." He got her to sit down on the couch in the very ordinary little living room and showed her one of the photographs. "Do you recognize this at all?"

She cleaned her glasses with her handkerchief and peered at it. "What's it supposed to be?—oh—" She studied it in silence and then said slowly, "Yes, I see—it's—it's part of a label, and it's just like the ones Rose had, the same kind of letters—and her name, that's got to be her name. She used to order them from a catalog, she made most of her own clothes, she loved to sew. Where—where'd you get this?"

Rodriguez told her gently, "From a body, Mrs. Larson. If you can identify that positively, I'm afraid it's your sister's body. She's been dead a long time."

She began to cry just a little. "I knew she had to be dead—she wouldn't just go off somewhere and not let me know. We were always close. Rose was a steady sort, a good woman, she wasn't impulsive or flighty—she had her regular routine, I always knew where she was and what she was doing. It was all so queer—coming back to find her gone, like that. Just gone. And nobody knowing anything! And finally Ed, my husband, said we'd better tell the police—and they found out she hadn't been in an accident or anything like that, but they couldn't find her."

"Back from where?" asked Maddox.

"Why, we'd gone back to Ed's old home town, Indianapolis. It was going to be his mother's and father's golden wedding anniversary, and there was a big family reunion. And we stayed over for nearly three weeks, because Ed was still getting over that accident with the car, he needed a rest, and there wasn't any reason to hurry back—he's got his own store, appliances and repairs— And when I couldn't get Rose on the phone, we went over to the apartment, and there was my letter and the postcards I'd sent her still in her mailbox, and she was gone."

"Didn't anybody there know anything?" asked Rodriguez.

"It's a big place, no manager there, she paid rent to a management company. She'd only lived there for six months, the other place got torn down for a new shopping center. She didn't know anybody there. And we asked at the dress shop, but she hadn't worked there long. You see, first she got a job at Sears, after Bert was killed, but she didn't like it, and she'd just gotten this job at the dress shop about a month before, she didn't know the woman who owned it very well. And all she could tell us was that Rose had called her and said she was quitting."

"She didn't say why?"

"No, and that wasn't like Rose. We couldn't understand it at all. She'd only worked since Bert was killed, he liked her to stay home."

"Bert was her husband?"

"That's right, yes. They were sorry they never had a family—but he didn't want Rose to work, he had a good job driving a truck, long trips across country—but it's a funny thing the way things happen, he wasn't killed on the job. He was just going down to the corner store for cigarettes, he wasn't even driving, when a car came around the corner and knocked him down and killed him. He was only forty-one. Rose took it pretty hard at first, but she was a sensible woman and she'd settled down to manage alone. But I know she'd been terribly lonely. Well, what I was going on to say, the police got permission to go into her apartment, and asked me to look—and all her things were gone. All her clothes, and her good dishes, and the portrait of Aunt Henrietta Winslow, and—well, everything! It was a furnished place, I mean the furniture was still there, but all Rose's things were gone."

Rodriguez smoothed his mustache. "She hadn't said anything to you about any changes she was thinking of making?"

"Not a word! I racked my brains at the time. There just wasn't anything I could think of. Why, the very last time I saw her—it was a Friday night, she usually came to dinner on Fridays, and we were starting back east the next day—she was just the same as usual. All I can remember is, she said it was awfully lonely coming home to an empty apartment, and I kidded her a little about finding a nice kind husband. She—"

"She didn't have a car?" asked Maddox.

"No, she never learned to drive. She sold Bert's car."

"She wouldn't have had much money, I suppose," said Rodriguez. "But the bank—"

"Oh, but she had Bert's insurance money. Ten thousand dollars. She hadn't decided what to do with it yet, it was in a savings account at the bank. But that was another thing the police found out. She took it with her. All her money, the ten thousand and the money in her checking account. She got a cashier's check for it. And that wasn't like Rose either. She was always careful about money," said Mrs. Larson. "We never could understand what happened—and now you're saying she's dead. But I knew she had to be."

There had been some paperwork to clean up, from a child molestation last week, and Sue and Daisy had just gotten through with that, filed one report and packaged the other for the D.A.'s office, at three o'clock. The only men in were Maddox and Rodriguez, for some reason doing a lot of telephoning; D'Arcy and Feinman had gone out on a new call, and everybody else was apparently out hunting heisters.

Daisy went down the hall for two cups of coffee, and they were sitting there taking a breather when a woman hesitated in the doorway and asked, "Are you detectives?"

"For our sins," said Daisy. "What can we do for you? Come in and sit down. I'm Sergeant Hoffman, this is Mrs. Maddox."

"Oh, I'm glad it's female police." She was looking indignant and grim; she was a pretty, dark young woman, smartly dressed in a tan dress with a beige raincoat over it. She sat down in the chair between their desks. "I thought the police had better hear about it. I was never so shocked or surprised in my life—and then of course I got mad. And my husband's going to say I was a damn fool and he just hopes I haven't picked up any bugs—so do I—but you have to do something about children, don't you? About babies. We've got two—Hugh and Linda—and I guess it was because of them, I went with that woman. I—"

"What woman? Can we have your name?"

"Mrs. Allan Glover. Nancy Glover." She gave an address on Lexington Avenue in West Hollywood. "I was a fool to come out without an umbrella, they were predicting more rain, but I just wanted to run up here to pick up my new glasses, the optician had called to say they were in. It wouldn't take half an hour. The office is at Hollywood and La Brea, and I left the car in a public lot on La Brea. And just as I came out of the building it started to come down, and I didn't even have a scarf. And I ducked under the awning of the first place across the street, to see if it'd let up in a few minutes." Sue offered her a cigarette. "Oh, thanks." She drew on it strongly. "Well, it didn't. And the place I was in front of was a liquor store, and this woman came up and looked in the window, just standing there. And I was just thinking I'd better make a dash for the car and risk getting absolutely soaked when she asked me if I wanted a baby."

"What?" said Daisy.

"Just like that. Yes. I asked her what she meant, and she said she was out of money and out of anything to drink at home, and she'd never wanted the baby anyway, it was a nuisance, and she'd sell it to me for enough to buy a fifth of vodka. I thought she was crazy—or drunk—but she wasn't. Not even drunk—just scruffy-looking. And I thought, my God, she really means it—and I thought, a *baby*—and so I gave her five dollars—and I drove her home. Home!" said Nancy Glover with a shudder. "My God. She went into the store and bought the vodka, and the rain let up about then and I said I'd take her home. I thought I'd better find out where she lived. It's a terrible place down on Delongpre—you never saw such a place! And a baby and two little children there—I was nearly sick—and she said I could have the other two for a ten spot. My *God*. And I thought the police ought to know."

Daisy said dryly, "Understatement of the week. Thanks very much for coming in, Mrs. Glover. What's the address? Did she tell you her name?"

Nancy Glover gave the address. "I didn't ask her."

"Well, we'll ask you to make a statement about this—at your convenience, come in any time—and you may have to tell the story to a juvenile-court judge."

"It doesn't matter—anything I have to do, just so those children are taken care of. Any place would be better. Allan's going to say I should have minded my own business, but you've got to do something about children." She stood up. "Will you do something right away? I hope so."

"We'll be on it," said Sue a little grimly.

She went out looking troubled, and Sue and Daisy went down the hall to the little office occupied by their Juvenile bureau. Elderly Sergeant Ralston was sitting there alone reading a paperback Western. They told him the tale, and he just said, "People."

They took his car to the address on Delongpre. It was a ramshackle tiny addition built onto an old single garage behind an equally dilapidated frame house in front. Ralston rapped on the door and in a minute it opened. He held out the badge.

The woman in the doorway was a redhead in her early twenties. She was already a little high on the vodka; she had the bottle in one hand. She was wearing torn green slacks and an overlarge sweat shirt. "What you want?" she asked in a slurred voice.

"What's your name, lady?" asked Ralston.

"Hartwig. Sally Hartwig. What's yours?"

"O.K., let us in, lady." He pushed the door wider open.

The little front room was nearly bare, and very cold. There was just a card table, two straight chairs, no rug, no curtains. Under the card table a baby about six months old was moving feebly, a very dirty baby minus even a diaper. Two older children, perhaps two and three, were just sitting on the floor. They hadn't many clothes on, and they were dull-eyed and stupid-looking.

"Are these your kids, Mrs. Hartwig?"

"Miss," she said, and hiccuped, and giggled. "Yeah. Couldn't tell you who their daddies were, I guess they're all mine."

Ralston said, "Not much longer, lady."

There wasn't a phone. Sue and Daisy kept an eye on her while he found the nearest pay phone and called Juvenile Hall. A squad arrived to take the children in half an hour later, and they took Sally Hartwig to the Wilcox Street jail and booked her in.

The only thing she said was, mournfully, "There's no lock on that damn door, some bastard'll get in and steal the rest of that bottle."

Maddox and Rodriguez had had the same thought at the same time. The banks. Where had Hinman banked? On the one hand, if he'd had a current account transferred, that would tell them where he'd gone; and on the other, there was Rose Parfitt's cashier's check. But there were a thousand banks all over town, and bank managers didn't open their records just for the asking.

"I'll be damned if I'm going to visit every bank in L.A. County personally," said Maddox.

"For openers," said Rodriguez, "central Hollywood and Long Beach."

"And that gives us at least a hundred," said Maddox exasperatedly. Feinman was there when they got back to the station, and they brought him up to date, got out the phone book and made a list, and started phoning. It was a tedious job, getting past underlings to the bank managers, explaining, asking them to hang up and dial back to verify that this really was the police. Asking them to check their back records: had a Charles Hinman ever had an account there? To four or more years back, or—in the case of Long Beach—recently? If so, had it been transferred to another bank? The answers wouldn't be forthcoming quickly, and they'd just have to keep plugging away at it until they found the right bank, or banks.

They hadn't, by the time the shift was coming to an end. D'Arcy came back at four o'clock and said the new call was another damn-fool kid dead of an O.D. There wasn't any I.D. on him; he'd been found by the manager in a cheap room at the kind of hotel where nobody was asked to sign a register. "The late edition of the *Herald*'s out," he added. "They're yelling about Snell loud enough for Sacramento to hear it without a radio."

"Three cheers," said Maddox bitterly. "Lock the stable door. Do you really think it'll do any good? How long is it since the state supreme court put back the death penalty, three or four years?—and nary a killer's been gassed since. Would you like to help out on some telephoning?"

"Not particularly," said D'Arcy. "What on?" Maddox told him. "For God's sake, we got one of those bodies identified? I'll be damned. But what are you thinking about—this fat middle-aged shoe clerk? Don't tell me."

"We've got a date now," said Rodriguez. "He was in that house when Parfitt vanished away. I know it's wild."

"Wild!" said D'Arcy. He leaned back in his desk chair and shut his eyes.

When they left at six o'clock, it was raining again. Maddox caught up with Sue at the back door onto the parking lot. She was struggling with a folding umbrella.

"Thank God tomorrow's my day off," she said. "And I know we need the two salaries, but my God, the things we see on this job— you'll never believe what went down this afternoon—"

"You can tell me about it at home." He opened the umbrella for her.

"It'll upset Mother."

"And for God's sake be careful driving in this deluge."

On Wednesday morning, Ellis came into the detective office just as everybody had gotten there and settled down. "The *Times* is in a tizzy," he said. "I haven't seen them so shook up since the editor went all tearful over that dopey who strangled the hooker. They're not talking about society being to blame, on Snell."

"Don't be maudlin, George," said Maddox. "Just climbing on the bandwagon." There was still a lot of telephoning to do to the banks. No sign of a lab report on Mainwaring. At least the night watch hadn't left them any new business. He would try the Ellingers again today, and that Joel Paxton. It never did any good to try to hurry the lab; they'd take their own time. The banks wouldn't be open until ten. And no kickback yet on that heister's description, from NCIC, so that was probably a lost cause.

But at a quarter to nine Baker came in with something. "The coroner's office finally sent that slug up, out of Mainwaring. It's out of a .22 Hi-Standard, a nearly new gun, hasn't been used much."

"Thank you," said Maddox. "We knew it was a small caliber. Do I dare ask when we can expect a report on what you got in that house?"

"There were a hell of a lot of latents," said Baker defensively. "Naturally, a big place like that. We had to get the wife's, the son's, the maid's prints, for comparison. We're still checking them. If we turn up any others, find out who else had been there lately and get theirs. We—"

"All right, all right," said Maddox. "You've got your own routine. Just get on with it."

"Franks may have something for you on that hit-run, he's been doing some analyses."

"Anything welcome." And when Baker had gone out, he suddenly thought of Charles Dickens. The eighteen-year-old homicide, if it had happened at all. The courthouse wouldn't be open until ten either.

Ellis had gone back to his office; now he came back and said, "I just had a call from the D.A.'s office, Ivor. They've set Snell's arraignment for Friday at ten A.M. The way I read it, they're anxious to get it over with and get him out of the limelight." He hunched his beefy shoulders, looking grimly pleased. "I don't think the public's going to forget this one in a hurry."

"Take no bets," said Maddox. It was nine-twenty, a decent time to reach the people in Beverly Hills—to reach Paxton. The phone shrilled at him and he swore and picked it up.

"You've got a new homicide," said Whitwell.

Maddox uttered one savage heartfelt obscenity.

CHAPTER 6

When Rodriguez and Feinman got there, it seemed it wasn't quite a homicide. "When I called in," said Patrolman Day, "I thought she was dead, and then I had another look and she's got a pulse, so I called an ambulance." They had time for about five minutes' look around before the ambulance arrived.

It was a beauty shop on Highland, a block down from Sunset, the Scissors 'n' Comb Shop. "It looks like a break-in," said Day. "Last night sometime, and the woman was working late and he walked in on her. The girl out there"—there was a blond girl weeping and wailing in the little anteroom—"one of the employees here, came to work half an hour ago, found the front door unlocked, came in and found her."

It looked like a fairly classy beauty shop. There was the carpeted anteroom with a little desk, modern upholstered furniture, a low table covered with magazines and, beyond a divider of amber plastic, rows of mirrored dressing tables with barber chairs along one side of a long narrow room, and on the other side a row of standard hair dryers, chairs, more tables with magazines. There was a woman's body sprawled in back of the first barber chair on the left: a tall thin woman with short dark hair, dressed in a white uniform. And some sort of struggle had taken place here: one of the hair dryers had been knocked over, one of the little tables, and there were magazines spilled all over the floor, bottles of hair rinse and shampoo evidently from the mirrored tables scattered on top of them.

"The girl just went to pieces," said Day. "I just got her name, Angela King, and the name of the woman, Leila Edwards." By the time the ambulance got there, the girl was in screaming hysterics, and the attendants gathered up both of them and took them off.

It looked like the run-of-the-mill break-in. At the back of the shop was a big utility room with shelves stacked with supplies, a back door onto an alley and public parking lot. The door was locked and bolted, but the window beside it was smashed in, and there was a hole big enough for a man to get through. Ten feet from the body of Leila Edwards there was a handbag upside down on the floor, contents spilling out of it, and no wallet visible. She had been here after the place closed, for some reason, and the burglar had broken in and surprised her.

There was a business license posted on the wall in the anteroom, in the name of May Reuther. On the desk was a big appointment book, and it had a handful of phone numbers scrawled inside the front cover: Reuther, Joyce, Claire, Linda. Rodriguez went out to the nearest pay phone to call, and Feinman glanced over the last couple of filled-in pages of the book. Yesterday's page showed only six appointments, and he thought vaguely that a shop like this, in a good central location and on a main drag, should be busier. Today's page listed seven appointments, the first at ten-thirty.

The lab truck hadn't arrived before Mrs. Reuther got there. She was a big rangy woman who had probably been a statuesquely good-looking girl thirty years ago; she had black hair with one arresting white streak in front, and she looked as if she'd thrown her clothes on hastily, not bothered to put on makeup. She said, looking around, "Oh, my God, this is all I needed. But you said she's not dead."

"She's seriously injured, I'm afraid," said Rodriguez. "She was one of your employees here, Mrs. Reuther?"

"My manager," she said. "I own the place, but I haven't been working here myself for over a year—my husband was very ill before he passed away, I had to be with him. Leila was running the shop—"

"How many employees do you have? The one who found Mrs. Edwards is the only one who's showed up."

She laughed sharply. "Angela King, yes, she's the only one here besides Leila. Business hasn't been so good lately, inflation catching up to us too—a lot of women are doing their own hair to save money, since we've had to raise prices. Do you think Leila's going to die?"

"We don't know, Mrs. Reuther," said Feinman patiently. "Would you look around to see if anything's missing?"

"I don't know what a burglar would find to steal here—you said he evidently got Leila's wallet. Oh—" Suddenly she turned and went over to the little desk, bent behind it. "And he seems to have gotten the day's take too, the cash box is gone. Damn." She described it, an ordinary steel box; they looked around the back room again and spotted it under the table beneath the broken window. It was empty. "How much might there have been in it?" asked Feinman.

"Depends on how many customers had been in," said May Reuther grimly. "I couldn't say. Leila always deposited the day's take at a night drop at the bank on her way home." The front door out there opened with a little rattle. "Damn, that'll be the first appointment—I'd better go and put her off—I suppose I'll have to close the place temporarily until I can come back and take over myself." She marched out to the front; they followed her, and she was briskly apologetic to the young woman who'd come in and who hurried out at finding the police on the premises.

"The shop usually closes at six?" asked Feinman. "It's not very likely somebody'd try the break-in until later than that. Ordinarily Mrs. Edwards wouldn't be here later?"

May Reuther said absently, "No, unless she stayed to do her own hair, or make up the books—sometimes she did that."

"Has she any family to be notified?"

"No—no, she's a divorcée, lives alone. I ought to go to the hospital, find out how she is. What a mess to clean up in there—" She sighed. "I can't see that anything's gone except the money, but I'd better get that window fixed, all the equipment's worth something."

"We'll probably be finished here in a couple of hours," Rodriguez told her. "We can't promise you we'll ever catch up to the burglar. It looks fairly anonymous."

"I don't expect so—burglars are a dime a dozen these days," she said tartly. "Well, I'd better get to the hospital, and find out about Angela too. Just the kind of silly girl who'd lose her head and go to pieces." She went out just as Garcia was coming in, and they left him starting to dust the window frame and went back to the station. Feinman began to type the report. Rodriguez called the hospital. Leila Edwards was still unconscious and likely to remain that way, in serious condition with a severe concussion.

Maddox was sitting in the very lush office of Joel Paxton, of Paxton, Dexter and Lynch on Elevado Avenue in Beverly Hills. He was thinking that he wouldn't trust Joel Paxton a yard, either as a lawyer or a man. Paxton was tall, dark and handsome, about forty-five, with a chiseled profile, an easy urbane charm, a resonant deep voice.

Of course, he had told Maddox, he was an old friend of the Mainwarings'; he had been deeply shocked to hear about the murder, it was a terrible tragedy for the family. He was sitting back in his leather desk chair uttering platitudes and making them sound original. Maddox interrupted him sharply.

"You picked Mrs. Mainwaring up on Saturday night and drove her to the party at the Ellingers'?"

"Yes, certainly." He smiled. "As you've probably heard, Charles loathed parties or going out anywhere, everybody had gotten out of the habit of expecting it. He was something of a loner, and Avis is—was used to that. It was just an informal evening, hardly a party. I dropped her at home at about eleven. But it occurred to me when I heard about the murder— God, it may have been lucky that Avis wasn't at home that night. Whoever shot Charles might have killed her too, if she'd seen—"

"On the other hand, Mr. Paxton, knowing he'd be home alone, Mr. Mainwaring might have arranged a meeting with whoever shot him. For some reason."

Paxton stared. "Oh, really, that never occurred to me—you think he knew the killer? That's rather farfetched, isn't it? Who'd have any reason to kill Charles? He wouldn't have been mixed up in any shady business deals, if you're thinking along that line. He was a man of very high principles."

"At any rate, you didn't go into the house with Mrs. Mainwaring?"

"No, it was late and she was tired."

"You're a bachelor, Mr. Paxton?"

His expression said that Maddox was overstepping authority. He said stiffly, "I'm divorced from my wife. If it matters. I can assure you that I hadn't any reason to murder Charles, if we're being farfetched, Sergeant."

"Well, it doesn't seem as if you could have, Mr. Paxton, when you were at a dinner party at the time he was probably shot," said Maddox evenly. "Who else was there?"

"Mr. and Mrs. Bell—Sylvia and Doug Bell—the Ellingers, Avis and myself. The Bells are old friends too, Doug is with General Oil."

"We're just checking generally on the facts. What Mrs. Mainwaring has already told us."

Paxton said meaninglessly, "Not at all. This is a damned awful thing for Avis, poor girl, she'll need friends to stand by her— But it does seem to me you're reaching, Sergeant, to imagine there was some personal motive. It's surely much likelier that some casual thief got in, and Charles surprised him."

"Both Mrs. Mainwaring and the maid," said Maddox, "say the house was locked back and front after dark, and there's no sign of a break-in."

"The maid!" said Paxton contemptuously. "That type would tell you anything you wanted to believe. If you want my opinion, she probably went off in a hurry on her night out, forgot to lock the back door and now she's feeling guilty about it. Well, I can only wish you luck in solving the mystery, not that it'll do Charles any good." He offered a well-manicured hand with a diamond ring on the third finger.

Maddox thought about Paxton on his way to the Ellingers' house on Cabrillo Drive. He also thought about Avis Mainwaring. People like these, not the kind of jet-set people who racketed around going through half a dozen marriages in a lifetime: well-bred people, upper-class society people, likely looking down their noses at the new-rich show-biz so-called sophisticated set. Civilized people, they'd accept the occasional divorce; and these days their moral standards were not as rigid as fifty years back. But Avis Mainwaring was a good-looking woman, and she must have found life a little dull and trying, damn all the money, with the loner who liked to stay home and read the classics, wouldn't even squire her to the occasional dinner party with friends. Mainwaring the upright businessman—and all business—not putting himself out for a mere wife. Mainwaring so proud of his distinguished ancestry, and— old-fashioned. Good-looking Avis, ten years younger, might have found Paxton a good deal more fun to be with. But if Mainwaring was as determined a loner as everybody said, maybe he'd just been relieved that somebody else was willing to squire his wife around. Innocently? Or had that marriage just declined into apathy, neither party caring a damn what the other did? Had Mainwaring had a girl friend on the side? And if so, who would know? He certainly hadn't been a man to confide in anyone, and he didn't seem to have had any close friends. There wouldn't be any record in his personal accounts of the rent for a little love nest somewhere; he'd be too canny for that.

The Ellingers' house was modern, window walls and stark furniture, and Evelyn Ellinger, though somewhere around Avis's age, call it late forties, looked modern too. She'd never been pretty; she had a pert, dark, gamin face, the pixie type, frankly platinum-tinted hair, long red nails, quick brown eyes. She was a chatterer. She told him all over again about the little dinner, about Charles hating to go out, about what a terrible mystery it was, and nobody could imagine it was anything but a burglar.

"I don't see what else could have happened, really—nobody had any reason to murder Charles. And I don't see why you wanted to talk to me—you aren't really checking up on Avis's *alibi,* are you? That's just silly."

"We have to go by the rules, Mrs. Ellinger."

"Frankly, I think it's a ridiculous waste of time, but anyway now you know she really was here—she and Joel got here about six-fifteen and they left around ten-thirty. So you needn't bother Sylvia and Doug to tell you the same thing. They're getting ready for a winter cruise and Sylvia will be just frantically busy."

Maddox wondered, starting the reluctant engine, whether that had been as casual as it sounded. The Bells lived on Seabright Terrace, another modern place, all angles; but nobody answered the door.

Feinman and Rodriguez were still up to their ears on the telephoning, and roped in Daisy to help. Traffic had called in two more daylight burglaries, and everybody else was out on that and the heisters. Feinman had just finished talking to the manager of a California bank in Long Beach when Communications sent up the kickback from NCIC on that description. All NCIC ever had in its computers were details of current crimes and currently wanted criminals. They had sent the details, descriptions and wants on four men who could conform to that description.

Terence Mackie, wanted for armed robbery in Waco, Texas. Jasper Ervin, wanted for armed robbery and homicide by New York. Curtis Henry Smith, wanted for rape and bank robbery by Colorado Springs. Daniel Cass, wanted for homicide—Feinman looked at the name twice, but it still said, sounding very unlikely, wanted by Yask, Montana. Well, he thought, better do something about this, and the sooner the better.

He went down to Communications and wired copies of the composite sketch to Waco, New York and Colorado Springs, but the fourth place defeated him. The girl at the board said, "Sorry, sir, there's no signal listed for such a place." Feinman went back to the office and looked up an atlas; there was such a place, a little mark on the map way northwest in the state. The nearest town of any size seemed to be a place named Libby. He dialed information, got the local operator—at least they had telephones—and asked for police headquarters.

The operator sounded surprised. "Police? There's just the sheriff. Sheriff Garrison."

"All right, give me his number."

"Oh, he just got back from Jeff's, his office is right downstairs, I'll connect you."

Sheriff Garrison had a warm slow voice with a little drawl. Feinman introduced himself, explained. "This is evidently a good composite sketch of the man, and it'd help to know for sure who he is."

"Composite?"

Feinman wondered if he'd heard of an Identikit. "But you haven't the facilities to accept a wired photo. Have you got a picture of Cass to compare?"

"Oh, anybody here'd recognize Dan Cass. Or Arnie."

"Well, where's the nearest place that's got a teletype board? There's a town called Libby, looks about the nearest one likely—is there one there?" The atlas credited Libby with around four thousand inhabitants.

The sheriff said, "Hell, no. I guess the nearest town you could send it to'd be Missoula. But we'd like to know where the Cass brothers are, all right. Look, you send your picture to Missoula, I'll run down there and take a look, probably get back to you tomorrow."

Feinman was looking at the atlas again. Somewhat aghast, he said, "But, my God, that's half the state away—it'll take you—"

"Oh," said Garrison casually, "I'll fly down, got my own plane half a mile down the road."

On Wednesday night there was only one call, a knifing in a bar. Both men were drunk. Both the dead victim and the killer turned out to be illegal aliens from south of the border. There wasn't anything for the day watch to do on that.

It was Maddox's day off.

Rodriguez and Feinman couldn't get back to calling the banks right away, until they were open, and with nothing new down sat talking about Hinman. Sue, who had heard all about it from Maddox, came back down the hall with a cup of coffee and stood listening.

"Just what are we thinking about here, Joe? That he went berserk all of a sudden and murdered the Parfitt woman for her cashier's check? And how did he come to know her? The sister had never heard of anyone named Hinman."

"It's even funnier," said Feinman, "when you remember the other body. I haven't settled on any theory—there are too many possibilities. It's just—funny."

"We can say that by all the evidence Parfitt went away voluntarily. She called the employer to quit her job, she went to the bank and took out the money, she packed her clothes to take."

"And," put in Sue, leaning in the doorjamb, "she was expecting her sister home soon, she probably meant to tell her all about it then—whatever change in her life-style she was making. But she never had the chance."

"It could be," agreed Rodriguez, "yes. And if so, that would pin it down to at least a three-week period. Only the rest of it's just a great big blank. Parfitt wasn't the kind to pick up a strange man, that's just ridiculous from what we know about her. And who the hell was the other one? We had hell's own luck in getting Parfitt identified, we'll never find out about the other one."

"And what about the wife at home?" asked Feinman. "Did she help him take up the floorboards in the closet and bury her? As D'Arcy says, this fat middle-aged shoe clerk—an eminently respectable citizen, just like Parfitt—"

"Dios mío," said Rodriguez suddenly, "I wonder if he's been murdered too."

"Now really," said Feinman, "let's not reach."

"Anybody could have written that damn letter. I doubt if McGuire would be familiar with his writing."

"That little idea," said Sue, "is even wilder than to think he went off the rails and committed murder."

"And I've just had an even wilder one," said Rodriguez. He looked a little excited. "So what about this wife?"

"What about her?" asked Sue.

"Is it possible she was a lunatic of some kind, Hinman covering it up —the reason he didn't talk about her—and she murdered Parfitt and he hid the body? Hid both the bodies after she poisoned them or—"

"I'll tell you, César," said Sue, "you and Joe ought to team up and try your hand at a mystery thriller. That makes about as much sense as—" Daisy called her and she went back across the hall. The phone rang on Feinman's desk.

"Say," said Sheriff Garrison's drawl, clear as a bell, "it's kind of silly but it gives me a damn funny feeling to pick up the phone and dial and be talking to you in Hollywood, California. I suppose it's nice and sunny and warm out there—"

"No, it's damn cold and looks like rain again. Have you seen the composite?"

"Yeah, I'm down here in Chief Pierce's office, I stayed over, they're predicting snow. It's Dan Cass all right, a damn good drawing of him too. I wonder what in time the Casses are making of Hollywood, California. Far as I know Dan and Arnie've never been fifty miles away from Yask."

"Well, we haven't got him, now we just know he's here. There are two of them you want? That figures—it's been a pair on all these jobs. What's the story on them?"

"Those Cass boys have always been fairly wild—the old man has a mighty thin little spread outside town, runs a few range cattle, they're dirt-poor riffraff. Dan and Arnie never got in any bad trouble, little hell-raising when they got drunk, that kind of thing. None of 'em likes to work very hard. But the whole thing surprised the hell out of everybody, and I reckon if I had picked up Dan and Arnie a lot of people around here'd all of a sudden got the lynch fever. Dan fell in love with the Potter girl—Francie Potter—which was just damn foolishness. Jase Potter's a big man, owns a big registered herd, couple thousand acres, and any of the Potters—including Francie—would about as soon have anything to do with the Casses as they'd go out and wallow in a sty with a bunch of hogs. Jase ran Dan off his place twice, and told him that in a little bit stronger talk, you get me. And a couple of days later Dan and Arnie showed up there when Jase was down state buying a new bull. Francie and her mother and a couple of hands were alone at the house, and Dan and Arnie killed all but one of the hands, and he'll be crippled for life. He told me who did it. It was a goddamned awful thing, they were cut to pieces with shotguns. The Casses got away in their dad's old pickup, we never got a trace of them."

"I see," said Feinman. "Well, they're here now. Have you got the plate number on the pickup? When was this, by the way?"

"About six weeks back. That won't help you any. The Idaho state police came across the pickup a week later, stalled outside Idaho Falls with a dead battery. You think you've got any chance of picking them up?"

"Let's hope we can, Sheriff. And thanks very much for the information."

When Sue got home on Thursday night she was looking tired. "It's a good thing," she said to Maddox and Margaret, dropping her raincoat in a sodden heap in the service porch, "that we're all modern and scientific and don't believe babies can be marked by prenatal experiences. Honestly, what a day! We had an attempted rape at a junior high school this afternoon, and the kid was thirteen—tried to rape one of the teachers in the gym. Daisy had to use some jujitsu on him. I hope you had a nice day off," she added to Maddox.

"I went looking at new cars. They all cost too damned much. And of course we both need one, but two sets of payments— You sure you're all right?"

"Don't fuss at her, Ivor. She's just tired," said Margaret.

"We can forget two sets of payments, with the baby coming. The Chrysler just needs a new battery. And I think I deserve a drink before dinner."

"Did the doctor say that's all right?" asked Maddox doubtfully.

"One can't do any harm. But I'm going to get into some dry clothes first," said Sue, heading for the stairs.

Maddox had gotten hold of William Sanford's secretary this morning and arranged to see him in his office at eight tonight. He had checked with Ellis this afternoon, and Ellis said no, there wasn't any lab report on Mainwaring in yet, but the autopsy report had come in, and there wasn't anything important in it except the estimated time of death, which was between eight and midnight. Maddox thought about that as he drove down the Glendale freeway. Midnight? If it had been as late as that, both women would have been at home—but in that big a house, with that small a gun used, they might not have heard the shot.

Sanford's office on Sunset, a solidly comfortable office at a good address, wasn't anywhere nearly as handsome as Mainwaring's. "Come in," said Sanford, hearing him in the outer office, coming out to meet him. "Sergeant Maddox?" He offered a hand. "Come in and sit down. My wife's mad at me anyway, I haven't had an evening at home in two weeks, so what's another?" He was a short plump man with sandy hair and friendly blue eyes behind glasses. "I was sorry as hell to put you off, but I really haven't had a minute." Maddox sat down in the client's chair and Sanford swiveled his desk chair around to face him. "They called to say Mrs. Mainwaring can claim the body. I'll be arranging the funeral tomorrow. What do you want to know? As I told you, I didn't know him well personally, or the family. I've never met the wife or son, never been inside his house."

"How did he leave the money?" asked Maddox. "I take it there's a will."

"Short and sweet," said Sanford promptly. "Half a million to the wife, the rest to the son. Both in trust, for her lifetime and until the son's thirty-five. That's his personal money. His entire interest in the business goes to the son, no strings. Gower owns about a third interest in the company."

"Like to quote some figures?"

"His own money, call it six million or so. The company, triple it."

"Good God almighty, that's a bundle. When was the will made?"

"Five years ago."

"No other bequests? Remembrance to devoted servants or whatever?"

"Nobody else is mentioned. He said there were only fourth cousins back east." Sanford hesitated and added, "Did you know the son was adopted?"

Surprised, Maddox said, "But for God's sake, he's the living image of the old man."

"That so?" Sanford was interested. "I understand he was the child of a first cousin of Mainwaring's. He told me—in strict confidence—because he wanted to be sure it wouldn't interfere with the will in any way. I was surprised he didn't realize that a legal adoption is as good as a natural birth, but he said they were putting in so damned many new rulings these days he thought he'd better tell me. It was a legal adoption, he went through a lawyer at the time. There's a family resemblance, is there?"

"Could he really be Mainwaring's son?" asked Maddox curiously.

Sanford laughed. "You wouldn't say that if you'd known Mainwaring. He was the coldest fish I ever ran across. The last man in the world to be a womanizer. I don't think he really liked women much. In any way. Just little things—the way he reacted to a slightly blue joke, for instance. And"—Sanford took his glasses off to polish them—"he told me something else, too, when he told me about the adoption. His wife had a child a couple of years after they were married—a son, completely retarded, hopeless case. Had to be put away in an institution, and died a few years later. She couldn't have any more children. I think—in a queer way—he may have blamed her, resented the fact that he couldn't have his own children."

"Oh, yes, I see," said Maddox. "Yes, a man like that— Do you know why he would have been writing you? He'd evidently just started a letter to you."

"Had he? No idea. He called me a week ago Wednesday and said he had a few matters he wanted to discuss, and we gave him an appointment for last Monday afternoon. He didn't go into any details, and it could have been anything to do with his personal affairs or the company's." Sanford cocked his head. "Which of them killed him, Sergeant? The wife—the son—the other man—or Gower? Gower was a lot less conservative in investments, Mainwaring had held him back from plunging more than once. He might figure he could manage the boy. Or is there a dark horse in the case?"

"At the moment," said Maddox slowly, "I'm not even guessing, Mr. Sanford." If that lab report ever came through—

At eleven-thirty the night watch got a call; Stacey and Donaldson went out on it. "Curson Street?" said Stacey. "Don't tell me, another mugging."

"They didn't say. We'll find out."

When they got up there, that was just what it was. Mr. Fred Wormser, whose wife was in the hospital recovering from surgery, had gone to visit her after dinner, and his sister and brother-in-law were there too, so after visiting hours they had gone out for a couple of drinks together. At, said Wormser, tenderly feeling the wet towel around his head, that new place where that really great combo was playing. He'd left there about ten forty-five and driven home, gotten out of the car in the drive to open the garage door, and this wild man jumped out of the bushes at him. An ape man, he said, a lot bigger than he was. "No, for God's sake, I couldn't describe him—I'm thinking about what color his hair is, while he's pounding my head on the cement? I was knocked out a couple of minutes, and no wonder—I come to and he's gone, the hell with the car, I got up and made for the house, called the cops." He hadn't, of course, seen which way the mugger ran.

"Did he rob you?"

"Certainly he robbed me, that was why he jumped me, wasn't it?" said Wormser irritably. "He got my wallet with about twenty-five bucks in it, and that's bad enough, but it's also got all my I.D., medical insurance card and credit cards and all those snapshots of the kids, no way to replace those, the negatives long gone. Hell and damnation."

"You'd better call the credit-card companies and report it," said Donaldson.

Wormser snarled. "Is that the most helpful thing the cops can think of? Certainly I will. But it's a goddamned nuisance."

About all they could do was write a report on it. But Stacey said, "It's the same block, Ken. That's three times. Somebody who lives around here?"

"Damn it, it's a fairly classy area. Nobody up here is exactly destitute."

"A juvenile—"

"Built like Tarzan, for God's sake? It doesn't make sense." The muggers usually lurked in parking lots, side streets up from main drags, and this lonely little residential street was six blocks up from Hollywood Boulevard. It wouldn't be once in a blue moon that anyone would be on foot up here—it was just her bad luck that Esther Cook had been.

It was just another funny thing.

On Friday morning, with Rodriguez off, Feinman got an unexpected call from a bank manager, at nine o'clock. His name was Kling, and he was the manager of a Security-Pacific bank in Long Beach.

"I'm glad to tell you, Mr. Feinman, that we've found that account you wanted to know about. The Hinman account."

"Fine. How long did he bank with you?"

"Actually it wasn't much trouble to locate—it won't go into the inactive file until next month, having been closed so recently. I've got all the dates and figures here for you. The account was transferred to our branch from a Hollywood branch on Vermont Avenue." And that, of course, wouldn't be far from the house on Ardmore. "That was, let's see, just two and a half years ago." When Hinman had gotten sent to the store in Long Beach from the one in Hollywood. "Do you want the amounts? At that time there was twenty thousand—in round figures— in a savings account, and five thousand in checking—"

"Right now," said Feinman, "I'm more interested to know when it got closed and what happened to it." Hinman had moved from the Long Beach address a week ago last Monday.

"The account was closed," said Kling, "a week ago last Wednesday. Mr. Hinman came in and arranged for his entire savings account to be transferred to a Crocker bank in Glassboro, New Jersey. It's all done by computer now, you know—"

"Yes. What about a checking account?"

"There was seven thousand four hundred and two dollars in the checking account, and he took three thousand in cash, a cashier's check for the rest."

"Well, thanks very much, Mr. Kling. We appreciate your cooperation."

"Not at all, sir. We have to cooperate with our police. What are you after him for?" asked Kling. "Has he committed a murder or what? Oh, I know better than to ask."

Feinman reflected thankfully that at least they knew where the man was, but it would be awkward to question him at long distance. It would be a little past noon in Glassboro, and he didn't think that was such a big town. He picked up the phone again and dialed information. D'Arcy, his lank length sprawled back in the desk chair, was on his phone and taking notes.

In three minutes Feinman was talking to a sergeant of detectives in Glassboro headquarters. He explained the situation and said, "It's possible he may have relatives there, or he'll be staying in a hotel, and he may already have been to the bank, given them an address."

"I get you," said the sergeant. "Give me the background on the homicide. We'll bring him in and question him."

"There's not a damn thing to hold him on. But we've got a date on the body, and he was living in the house then."

"I get you. We'll be in touch. You do get the offbeat ones in the glamor town, don't you?"

Feinman put the phone down, looking out the tall windows to the dark threatening sky; a cold gusty wind had gotten up and was howling eerily around the building. Maddox had left half an hour ago to cover Snell's arraignment downtown, and nobody else was in but Nolan, typing a report.

D'Arcy came over and perched a hip on the corner of the desk. "So at least we've found Hinman," he said. "That was the manager of a Bank of America in Long Beach. They located the account, Hinman banked there."

"What do you mean?" said Feinman. "I just—"

"He closed out the account last week, and had his savings account transferred to a Bank of America in Warrensburg, New York," said D'Arcy. "There was about four thousand in his checking account, and he took it in cash."

Feinman stared at him. "Say that again, will you?"

Maddox walked into the Hall of Justice at a quarter to ten. This was part of the cumbersome red tape, the machinery of the law, that police had to deal with. Most detectives passively resented the necessity of spending the time at it, but it was part of the job.

He had photocopies of all the reports on the Kelsey case; they probably wouldn't be needed, but you never knew about judges. Usually, an arraignment took about ten minutes.

The press was out in force. Ever since it had broken for the press, on Tuesday, they hadn't let up on it. Already the letters to the editor would be coming in, starting to get printed today and tomorrow. The TV talk shows nationwide were loud with acrimony one way and the other. In the little bare courtroom the judge was already on the bench, looking bored and sleepy, and nobody else was there but the press and a couple of bailiffs—a lot of the local press, photographers with their Speed Graphics, three TV crews with movie cameras, and he even noticed a few from *Time* and *Newsweek*.

The bailiff came in suddenly through the little door at the rear of the courtroom, like a jack-in-the-box popping up. He had Henry Snell by one arm. Snell looked bored too. And Maddox had a sudden sickening flashback, to when he'd talked to Roy Kelsey about Snell.

"This scum—this filthy stinking scum—and Bobby with his whole life in front of him," Kelsey had said dully. "I can't stand to think about it—I don't know why God would let it happen, if there is a God."

The big crowd of press surged forward, and the cameras started to click and hiss. The judge woke up and looked annoyed. Maddox was behind the crowd of press men. "Bailiff!" said the judge, and banged his gavel. "I won't have this disturbance—"

The gun spoke before anyone realized it was a gun firing. The little splats were flat and hard, and stopped in ten seconds. Somebody shouted, and the crowd of press shifted and surged forward. "Bailiff!" cried the judge, and Maddox shoved the nearest men aside and plunged past the tangle of people. A fat man with a press card on his lapel was panting, "It was him, he did it, I saw him," and he was pointing at another man, and the crowd fell back on either side and Maddox reached out and took hold of Roy Kelsey's arm.

One bailiff was running up the corridor, probably to yell for an ambulance. Snell wouldn't need an ambulance. He was sprawled flat on his back, arms and legs wide, on the floor in front of the judge's bench, and there was a slowly spreading puddle of blood around him.

For a moment there was a strange moment of absolute silence.

Roy Kelsey held out the gun to Maddox. "It's all right," he said in an empty voice. "I won't make you any trouble, Sergeant. I've done what I meant to do. I hadn't fired a gun in years, but I used to be a pretty good shot." He was wearing a felt hat with a sign stuck in the band that said PRESS. "After all the stories in the papers—and they said when he'd be brought up in court—I figured I could get near him this way." He gave Maddox a taut little grin. "You guys—were nice to me. Thanks. Look, it's Nick's gun—I knew where he keeps it under the counter. You see he gets it back, will you?" He looked at Snell on the floor. He said, "It doesn't matter what you do to me. But that filthy scum, he'll never murder anybody else's kid ever again now."

CHAPTER 7

They got Maddox's call at the station at ten forty-five; it was relayed up to Feinman. "It's a madhouse here, the press is going wild and the Central homicide boys flocking around. The judge looked as if he'd like to send everybody to jail including the bailiffs. The Central boys would like to shake Kelsey's gun hand and let him go, only of course it doesn't work like that. I don't know when I'll get back, there's miles of red tape to tie up."

"I can see that," said Feinman. "There's something to be said about Mosaic law, isn't there? It's final. We get told to leave vengeance to the Lord, but I guess we can all understand how Kelsey felt. We'll expect you when we see you. There's something just breaking here too." He told D'Arcy and Nolan about it, went across the hall to tell Sue and Daisy. "And now, what the hell is all this about Hinman and his bank accounts?" He and D'Arcy had been putting the facts together when Maddox called. "By God, César's going to be interested in this, I think I'll call him."

Rodriguez was so interested that he said he'd come in.

"So he wasn't putting all his eggs in one basket," said D'Arcy. "But will you tell me where the hell he got all the money? Working for that shoe chain for years, I wouldn't think he could save up that much."

"He could be a gambler, though we haven't heard that, and he doesn't sound the type. But there would have been ways. If he was in the market—not the big stocks, the little stuff you can get for twenty, forty bucks—especially back all those years, he could have piled up the nest egg."

Rodriguez, coming down in a hurry, heard about Snell and Kelsey almost impatiently, looking at the scrawled notes on the two bank accounts. "Warrensburg, New York. So we don't know where the hell he's gone. Either place. Going back to where he'd lived as a young man! So we'd better get that force to look for him too. And he'd worked in a good many places for Lester's, as McGuire said—you know," said Rodriguez reflectively, smoothing his mustache, "I get the impression he has gone off the rails, if not before, just now. The very steady reliable businessman, living by ordinary humdrum routine, and all of a sudden he quits the job, isn't sure where he wants to go, feeling nostalgic for his youth. It sounds as if he'd just found out he has an incurable disease, and he's dropping out of everything to spend his last days in a place where he'd been happy and contented before."

"That's exactly what it does sound like," said D'Arcy, struck. "Just dropping out of the rat race."

Feinman was on the phone to New York. "And I'll tell you something else," said Rodriguez. "I think it'd be a good idea to get on the wire to Lester's main headquarters, get them to look up his record and tell us every place he had worked. He might be intending to visit several youthful scenes before settling down. Look at the amount of cash he took."

He got onto that himself; it would take Lester's a while to look up that record, with the number of employees they must have, and it was now half-past two in New York. He wrestled with the switchboard girl, with various clerks and secretaries, and finally achieved contact with an efficient-sounding Wilbur Stanley in the personnel office, who listened intelligently. "I see. You think the man may be concerned in a serious crime—not pleasant to hear about one of our old employees, Mr. Rodriguez—and it's possible he may have gone to any of several places he has worked before. I can certainly have his file looked up for you."

"Anyplace back east. He's transferred funds to Glassboro, New Jersey, and Warrensburg, New York. If he'd lived anywhere else in those states, or even a little farther away—"

"Yes, I see. Well, we keep a complete file on all our employees, and by what you tell me the man has only recently resigned from the company, his name will still be in our file of current employees. That would be the master file here—the regional offices would only have—"

"That's why I'm calling you," said Rodriguez patiently.

"Yes, of course. I'll put a couple of girls onto it at once. I'll hope to get back to you by tomorrow."

Rodriguez swung away from the phone. Feinman had just finished talking with the police in Warrensburg. "They say they'll get right on it. But I ask you, what the hell can we say now on Parfitt? Does this take us any farther into that? That money—and Parfitt and her cashier's check?"

"It's up in the air," said Rodriguez, "but I can think of a way he could have met her. That shoe store in Hollywood is in the same general area where she lived and worked. They could have gotten into casual conversation, at a coffee shop, or waiting for a bus—*Dios,* hasn't anybody checked on a car? Hinman must have had a car, damn it—"

"Naturally I checked with Sacramento," said Feinman. "Didn't I tell you? There's nothing registered to him now. But you know how the paperwork gets done there. He could have changed cars a couple of months ago, turned something in, and the registration's not on file yet. Didn't you ask, on all your researches on him?"

"Mea culpa," said Rodriguez. "I didn't. We'd better." He called Fenton in Long Beach, and found him in.

Fenton said, "Why, yes, he had a new Chevrolet sedan. When they moved in here he was driving an old Ford, it died on him about a year ago, just worth junking, and he went without a car after that, took the bus. But when he got transferred to the new store, he went and bought a car. That was just two weeks before he moved out. I don't understand why you're asking all these questions about him, I must say."

Answers, thought Rodriguez, lighting a new cigarette. Naturally the registration wouldn't be on file in Sacramento yet. "Do you know where he bought it?" Fenton didn't, and there were at least twenty different agencies around Long Beach where he might have gone. Rodriguez started calling them. He hadn't found the right one when D'Arcy and Feinman suggested lunch, and he realized with surprise that it was one-fifteen and he was hungry.

Waiting for sandwiches at the coffee shop in the next block, he said, "Places he could have met her. Parfitt. Casually. Look—the wife. We don't know anything about her. She could have met Parfitt as a customer at that dress shop, for instance."

"All right, that's plausible," said D'Arcy, "but where do we go from there?"

Feinman said suddenly, "And all that money—I'm getting another impression— That he's a miser. Greedy for money. Maybe lucky about money—gambling on investments. To have parlayed a clerk's salary— even a manager's salary—into that kind of money, even over thirty years, he must be pretty damn tight-fisted and shrewd, and for all we know the wife was the same way."

"Are you building a story?" asked Rodriguez.

"I think so. The wife met Parfitt, and Parfitt came visiting the house, they got to be casual friends, and the Hinmans found out about the insurance money she had. Say Hinman got her believing he could give her good advice on investing it, promised to double it for her, got her to get that cashier's check—"

"Which could be traced down in time," said D'Arcy.

"If she cashed it herself?" countered Feinman. "She's going to invest the money on something he's sold her on—"

"But she voluntarily quit her job and moved," said D'Arcy. "Why?"

"Not necessarily. All we know she did was to get the money from the bank. The rest would be easy. Her employer didn't know her well. The wife could have made that phone call. They'd have her keys, they could clean out the apartment at their leisure."

After a silence, Rodriguez said, "And what about the other one?"

"Maybe it wasn't the first time they'd done it."

The sandwiches came. D'Arcy said, "Well, by God, that at least hangs together, Joe. That kind do exist."

"Seddon," said Rodriguez ruminatively. "The same exact type. Murdered the old lady renting a room in his house, for her money. And that was a poisoning case. If that's the way it was, they were damned lucky Parfitt hadn't mentioned them to her sister. Of course, he could have spun a tale, keep the wonderful investment secret for some reason —and of course they'd pick the period when the sister was away, to give themselves time. All I can say is, if that's so, the fat little shoe clerk must be one hell of a persuasive talker, but the unlikeliest people are."

"And now he's feeling remorseful?" asked D'Arcy.

"I could imagine a little story on that too. The wife's now dead and maybe he's lonely. Maybe he's just realized that the money's not everything, can't give him back his youth. Maybe he really has got cancer or something, and that's why he's dropped everything and faded out."

"The way we said." D'Arcy nodded. "Yes. Well, if that's so, maybe when we do locate him he'll come right out with the story."

Sue and Daisy had just gotten back from late lunch when a woman came in with a little girl. She was a thin woman, perhaps forty, with mousy hair, dressed rather dowdily. She introduced herself as Mrs. Anderson. "I had to bring Ann to see you, but I think I'd better talk to you privately before you talk to her," she told Daisy. She looked worried and upset. The girl was about twelve, a plain-faced brown-haired girl in blue pants and tunic and a quilted car coat. She'd been crying. Sue raised her eyebrows at Daisy and shepherded the girl down the hall to sit under the fatherly eye of Sergeant Ralston, and came back. Mrs. Anderson said, "It's a dreadful thing, but we know it does happen, and oftener than we like to think, too. I teach at Le Conte Junior High, and Ann's in my home room—Ann Fogel. I've suspected

there was something wrong, the way she's looked and acted, and a couple of her regular teachers I know have said her work has fallen off a
lot. I could see she'd been crying when she came into my room today,
and well, I like to help the children as I can, and I was worried about
her—she's quite a nice girl—I got her to stay afterward, and ques-
tioned her, and it all came out. These drunken bums—it's the father,
he's been abusing her sexually for months, and she's tried to tell her
mother but the mother won't believe her."

"Oh, Lord," said Daisy. "Yes, it happens oftener than most people
know."

"I don't know how you handle this sort of thing, but I had to bring
her in and tell you."

"Do you know her address, anything about the family?" asked Sue.

"No, I'm afraid not. I got the address for you from the files, I had to
get the principal's permission to skip my last class, and told him."

"Well, the first thing we do is get her medically examined," said Sue.
"If it's true—and we also get the kids telling lies about their parents,
you know—we go on from there."

"I—just leave her here with you? She's so scared—" Mrs. Anderson
was a nice woman.

"You can go with her to the hospital if you like," said Daisy.

"I think I'd better."

They got the girl in and talked with her, and she sounded authentic
—embarrassed, scared, tearful. "I tried to tell Mom, but she just says
I'm wicked to tell lies—and she won't believe me. About him. It's got
so I'm scared to go home—because Mom works nights, and he's always there—and he's always gettin' drunk, it's when he's drunk he—
you know—does it to me—he don't have a job since he got fired from
the gas station—and Mom won't listen and I—"

"Everything's going to be all right. You were smart to tell Mrs. Anderson," Daisy told her. "Now, we're going to take you to see a doctor
—you're not afraid of doctors, are you?" She shook her head. "They'll
be nice to you. And then we'll decide what to do next." Sue was on the
phone to the emergency wing at Cedars-Sinai.

They had to wait at the hospital for a doctor to be free. He had a
look at the girl and said she'd been raped all right, repeatedly, and
knocked around a little.

It was five-thirty then and Sue called the station to find out if Maddox was back. He'd just come in. "Listen, Ivor, I'm stuck with some
overtime here," and she explained. "We've got to wait for the doctor to

sign a report, you know all the red tape, and take the girl down to Juvenile Hall and check her in, and apply for the warrant on Fogel. I
can't possibly get home until seven-thirty at least. Will you call Mother
and tell her?—and just to fix some soup or something, I'm not very
hungry anyway."

"We've both had a day," said Maddox. "Tell you what, would you
settle for a nice big club sandwich?"

"That sounds fine."

"O.K., I'll wait for you here and we'll go out. To that place on Fairfax, and listen to the nice music over the sandwiches."

They had the club sandwiches, and stayed on, listening to the music,
over more coffee. The four old men on the little platform were enjoy-
ing making the music as much as the audience enjoyed listening. They
hadn't forgotten anything about making the music. The piano player
did some fancy things to "The Spell of the Blues," on a first chorus,
and then the sweet tenor sax took over on smooth improvisation. They
went on to "Temptation," and "Dinah," and "Once in a Blue Moon,"
and "Please." The fat white-faced drummer could make his marimba
talk. And old Claude Delarue was obviously having the time of his life,
finding out the people still liked them, knew them for the best. His
round black face gleamed with perspiration, beaming on the people between numbers. They played "If I Had You" and "Let's Do It" and
"S'posin'" and "May I?" and "Paradise" and "Blue Prelude." The
place was packed, and the people loving them, not just because they
were good but also because they loved the music too and respected it.

When Sue went to the dressing room, Maddox went over to the platform. "Would you like to do a request for my wife?"

Claude Delarue said amiably, "Sure, man. What'd you like?"

"Couple of choruses of 'Sweet Sue'?"

"Right on, man. Some special celebration, maybe?"

"You could say so. A first baby."

Delarue's face broke into a wide white grin. "Man, that's nice, real
nice. Ellie May and I only had the one, we'd have liked more, and
what do you know, he grows up to be a big important doctor. Funny as
all hell, me barely gettin' out of grade six and Ellie May not much better." He gave Maddox a friendly wink. "Good luck to both of you—we
do a real sweet arrangement for the little lady." They did, the golden
voice of the sax effortless and pure. Maddox and Sue sat and held
hands and he asked, "You feel better?"

"A thousand percent better, darling. I can face another day now. Most ways you're a very satisfactory husband."

Feinman was off on Saturday. When Maddox came in, Rodriguez and D'Arcy wanted to talk about Hinman, the queer things that were showing up on that, and it was a funny one, the way it was breaking. But what Maddox was chiefly interested in was the lab report on the Mainwaring house, in at last. He studied it with interest and passed it on to D'Arcy. "So now we can make a few deductions. And ask some questions. Her prints were on the phone in the study, on the desk, and also on the dial of Mainwaring's wristwatch. The son's prints were on the desk too, and he left all ten of his prints, and palm prints into the bargain, on top of the desk opposite the desk chair—as if he was leaning there facing Mainwaring. Interesting." There was a lot more, about prints through the rest of the house, but that didn't say much.

"So she never went into the study?" said D'Arcy. "But if she did it, it was after she got home. And the maid would have heard her drive out. What did she do with the gun? Where did she get the gun?"

"We didn't dig up the backyard. We may have to. There's been something at the back of my mind—they were all so casual about it, but dinning it into us so we wouldn't forget it, what time she and Paxton left the dinner party. And now we knew, we needn't go bothering the Bells. I think before we talk to Avis we'll talk to Sylvia Bell."

They found her home this time, in the angular house in Beverly Hills; and she looked at the badges as if they were twin snakes. She was a little round soft fluffy-haired woman with a foolish slack mouth, and she said with a gasp, "My husband's just down in the den watching the football game, I'll get him—"

Maddox had no desire for a probably masterful husband; he steered her gently into a living room full of Danish modern furniture, saying casually, "I don't think we need to bother him, Mrs. Bell, we've got just a few questions about that little party a week ago tonight, at the Ellingers'." She sat on the edge of her chair and twisted her hands together tightly.

"What—do you want to ask?"

"Let's see, you all got there about six-thirty, and you just sat talking after dinner, and what time was it you left?"

"Doug and I left about ten-thirty, and Joel and Avis were getting ready to leave then."

"Oh," said Maddox doubtfully. "Is that so?" He looked at D'Arcy. "That wasn't what that maid said, was it?"

"I'd have to look up my notes, but I thought it was earlier she said Paxton and Mrs. Mainwaring—"

"No, it wasn't," Sylvia Bell broke in. "No, we all left together, the maid wouldn't know anything about it."

"There was a maid serving the dinner?"

"Oh, yes, but she was out of the house by nine o'clock, Evelyn said so, and it wasn't until nine-thirty we went out to—" She stopped dead. "Oh, my God. I told Evelyn not to trust me, I'm such a fool about telling lies—"

Maddox beamed on her kindly. "It's always better to tell the truth, Mrs. Bell. You went out where? All of you? At nine-thirty?"

She sniffed into a handkerchief. "It doesn't mean anything," she said wretchedly. "It was just, Avis said it would be better—the way it *looked,* but everybody knew Charles never went anywhere, and just because Avis and Joel—well, it isn't important, but Evelyn said least said soonest mended, and so did Doug—when we knew about Charles—"

"So it doesn't matter if you tell us, does it?" said Maddox. "Where did you go?"

She sat up a little. "Evelyn wanted to go dancing somewhere. So we all went down to Angelo's, but Joel didn't like the combo—and he and Avis went on somewhere else—they'd come in his car."

"At about ten o'clock?" asked Maddox. She nodded. He looked at D'Arcy, who rounded a thumb and forefinger at him silently.

"This might give us some interesting ideas," he said to D'Arcy as they waited for Avis Mainwaring. They had sent a squad for her, just to let her know there'd be no pussyfooting around, obsequious cops and upper-class lady. "But if it was either of them, separately or together, it wasn't planned. They wouldn't have known that the dinner party would end up at Angelo's, giving then an excuse to leave early. And I'll bet you it's been on the grapevine in all that set, Avis and Joel making a pair. I can think of this and that. She and Paxton did a little smooching saying good night, and Mainwaring heard them—I can hear him saying, come down to the study, my dear, we must discuss this, really can't have my wife behaving so indiscreetly—or saying it to both of them—and maybe there was a row. Hot words."

"And Paxton had the gun on him?"

"Mainwaring had one gun in his desk. Maybe he had two. The little one as well. He'd just started to write a letter, maybe the drawer was open, where the gun was."

"You taking any bets on which it was?"

"I'd go for Paxton, if he's got enough temper to lose—a very cold cautious gent—she seems to go for the type. He'd probably be quite willing to take on a wife with money, but he'd rather do it by divorce, not murder. In fact, she'd have gotten a hell of a lot bigger divorce settlement than she gets by that will. But if they were having a row anything could have happened."

The uniformed man brought her in presently and they took her down to one of the cramped little interrogation rooms, just for the atmosphere. She sat down at the bare little table in silence, but her mouth looked taut. "So," said Maddox pleasantly, "Mrs. Bell gave the game away and we know about Angelo's. And that you and Paxton left the party earlier than you claimed." Her mouth tightened and her eyes looked wary. She was in conventional black again today, very smart. "Does the general gossip agree that you're Paxton's mistress, by any chance?"

"You needn't insult me," she told him evenly, "just because my husband was murdered. I told Evelyn it was a silly idea, we ought to tell the truth. There wasn't any reason not to. Except for that, everything I told you was the truth."

Maddox smiled at her. "Oh, not everything, Mrs. Mainwaring. You said you seldom went into your husband's study, but we found your fingerprints there. On the telephone—"

"Well, I didn't mean I never went there—"

"And on the dial of his wristwatch."

"Oh!" she said, and her eyes flickered.

"You were there that night. We'd like to hear the whole truth this time."

"Aren't I allowed to have a lawyer with me when you're asking questions?"

"Certainly," said D'Arcy. "We can postpone this until you get one, if you'd like. But we'll still be asking the questions."

"You'd just better tell us the truth, Mrs. Mainwaring. Do you want to wait for an attorney?"

She shook her head and sat up straighter. "No. It doesn't matter. It doesn't mean anything, I was just—frightened and nervous. I lost my head, that's all."

"So what happened? After you and Mr. Paxton left Angelo's, where did you go?"

"Nowhere—important," she said, head bent. "Joel didn't want to go dancing. We went—to a place on Beverly, the Giaconda Club, and had a couple of drinks, and then Joel brought me home."

100   SKELETONS IN THE CLOSET

"What time?"

"About midnight. A little later. He didn't come in. He let me off and I went in—"

"Was the front door locked?"

"Yes, of course. And I saw the study light on, and I went down there to—to tell Charles he shouldn't sit up so late"—she was nervous on that, and well she might be—"and there he was. Dead. I was frightened. At first I thought he'd shot himself, only Charles never would, and then I saw there wasn't any gun. I felt his wrist—to see if he was dead—and I picked up the phone to call the police, and then I didn't. I was so frightened—and I was tired—it all seemed just too much. I don't think I knew what I was doing, really—I just went upstairs and went to bed. I admit it was very silly and foolish, but women sometimes are." Her voice was shaking as much as her hands now. "I thought—I could face it better in the morning. That's all."

"Did he keep a second gun in his desk?" asked Maddox.

"I don't know. I'm afraid of guns."

"Who were you going to call, besides the police? Or instead?"

"Just—the police. I can't—"

"Paxton? Or was he right there with you, had he used the gun? And you were going to call Evelyn Ellinger to arrange that story, you were still there at ten-thirty."

"No!" she almost shouted at him. "No, I was alone—that was why I was frightened—"

"Did you have an argument with him? What time did you really get home, Mrs. Mainwaring?"

"Just—when I told you. And I—"

"And why were you so frightened? Just of a dead body? Why didn't you call the police?"

She dropped her hand from her mouth, and her eyes looked a little wild. She lashed out at him, "Because I thought it was Jim, you fool! After that fight he had with Charles on Friday night, I thought he'd done it—and I couldn't have cared less! And I'm not going to answer any more questions without a lawyer present."

On Saturday morning Rodriguez finally turned up the Chevy agency where Hinman had bought the car. They could give him the temporary license number; they also told him that Hinman had paid for it in full with cash, which had struck everybody as a nine days' wonder. And so it would have. He put out an A.P.B. on the car and Hinman, as an empty gesture; they knew that Hinman had probably left the state.

It was just before noon when Stanley at the personnel office in New York called him back, and Rodriguez took down the information as he relayed it. It made depressing reading. When Lester's had first hired Hinman twenty-nine years ago, he had worked in the store in Glassboro. Three years later he had moved to a store in Warrensburg, New York. He had stayed there for seven years. Nineteen years ago he had moved to a store in Glens Falls, New York. And three years later he'd been transferred to a store in Corinth. He had been there until, for whatever reason, he was transferred clear out to California, ten years ago. And here he had worked all over the L.A. area, in six or seven stores. Rodriguez thought, better get in touch with Glens Falls and Corinth.

He had talked with the police in Glens Falls and was about to dial information again when Franks came in. "I've got something a little interesting for you. On that hit-run where the little girl was killed. There were a few flecks of paint on her clothes, from the car—probably where she bounced and hit the hood—he must have been traveling damn fast. I've been doing some analyses—matter of fact, you'd probably have got that lab report on Mainwaring quicker if I hadn't gotten interested in this. The paint is the kind that's been used on all Pontiac models the last three years. It's royal blue. I don't know if it'll give you any useful leads, but it narrows it down some."

"It could. That must have been one hell of a job."

"Interesting," said Franks.

Rodriguez got Corinth and talked to police headquarters there. The sergeant he talked to said both the detectives and the chief were out somewhere, but he sounded intelligent and took down the information accurately.

Maddox and D'Arcy had gone to look for Jim Mainwaring, but he wasn't at home— "Walking on the beach at Malibu!" said Maddox. Paxton was absent from home and office. They tried the *Herald* office and asked for Rick Hyatt, and found him at a scarred old desk at the far end of a big communal office. He was a heavy-shouldered dark fellow about Jim's age, probably a very junior reporter, and he was perfectly polite but he wouldn't answer any questions.

"Jim's a good friend of mine," he said, "and I don't go tattling on a friend's personal affairs. You can prod at me all you want, you don't use the third degree these days, it won't do you any good." He did tell them that he'd had dinner with Jim at the Italian restaurant in Beverly

Hills, a week ago tonight, and that Jim had mentioned going on to that movie.

It was about the end of the day. They went back to the station, and met Sue and Daisy just driving in, in Daisy's Pontiac.

"We finally picked up that Fogel, and he was drunk, so we can't talk to him until tomorrow," said Sue. "His wife still doesn't believe it, she's saying the girl's in some trouble with a boy at school and just telling nasty lies. I feel as if I need a bath." The day men were drifting out to the parking lot.

Garcia paused beside the four of them there, dangling his car keys in one hand. "You haven't gotten back to me about that report. I thought it was a little interesting myself."

"We've been busy. What report?"

"That beauty shop the other day."

"Oh," said D'Arcy, "that break-in. Did the victim die, by the way?"

"No," said Maddox absently. "César checked again yesterday—she was still unconscious but they're saying she'll make it. I didn't see your report."

"I left it on your desk. Have a look at it."

"Tomorrow."

It had stopped raining, but had again turned bitterly cold: pure air direct from the new snow on the back mountains was sweeping over the whole Los Angeles basin.

The night watch was geared up for Saturday night, but again it was a fairly quiet night. Maybe the cold was keeping people indoors. They got called out at nine-thirty to an attempted rape in a parking lot on Santa Monica. The girl had fought him and gotten away, run to the drugstore on the corner. She was all right except for being scared, and she couldn't give them any description, just that he was young and black and talked dirty to her. She'd been lucky. Donaldson told her she ought not to be out alone even at that hour, and she said bitterly, "You don't think it's my choice, do you? But we all take turns at evening shift the nights the store stays open."

A heist went down almost as soon as they got back, and it seemed to be that pair again, now identified as Dan Cass and probably his brother Arnie. At least the two witnesses said they were both blond and big, and probably if Stacey or Brougham had had a copy of the composite sketch along, they'd have identified it. This time the bunglers had been slightly more successful; they had more sensibly picked a liquor store, a very small one, on Virgil. The owner had been there alone with a clerk, and as usual Saturday had been a pretty good day, he said. He thought there might have been about four hundred dollars in the register.

"We'd like you to come in and look at a picture," said Stacey.

"All right, but that don't get me my money back. My wife's pestering me to get out of this business, all the holdups and being out late with criminals all around. Hollywood used to be a nice clean town—but these days, the hookers out in broad daylight, and the dirty movies advertised right out, right on the boulevard. It's a disgrace."

He was, of course, quite right. Brougham was thirty-one, Stacey only four years older, but even they could remember when Hollywood had been a nice clean town.

The next call came in just after the Traffic shift changed at midnight. When they got to the address, on Gardener Avenue, it was a church: a modest little white frame church with a narrow front porch. The sign over the door, faintly visible from the light at the corner streetlight, said Church of the Brethren. The patrolman was Bob Leroy, and he said, "It isn't exactly a felony, but I know the front office has been working on it off and on, and I thought you'd be interested." The front door of the church was open.

Inside, in the small foyer, were four people: a large and broad young man with an open, good-humored face, a pretty, dark girl and two kids about fourteen. "Mr. and Mrs. Brock Calloway," said Leroy. "The detectives would like to hear the story, Mr. Calloway."

"Sure. Like I was just telling you, I guess it means we go back in the car again awhile, but it can't be helped. See, Becky and I came down here," he started telling them obediently, "from Fresno, when I lost my job when the plant closed. We heard there were more jobs open down here, and we had nearly five hundred bucks saved up, keep us going until we got jobs. We been here about three weeks, I been to the employment agency every day, and I got a job at an assembly plant but it doesn't start till next Monday. We was staying at a motel, but it was awful high. Anyways, last Monday I had my wallet stolen—it must've been one of these pickpockets, and pretty slick too, I never felt anybody touch me. It had all our money in it except for about forty dollars Becky had in her purse."

"So we checked out of the motel," said the girl, "and we figured we could just about make it, eating kind of slim, and maybe Brock could get a salary advance if he told the new boss what happened. We stayed in the car a couple of nights, but it was so cold and rainy—"

"Like to get pneumonia," he said, giving her an affectionate smile. "It was Becky's idea, a church. We thought most churches'd be left open, but they don't seem to be, till we found this one, last Thursday. We've been coming in late, leave the car in the lot out there, and sleeping in the minister's office, I guess it'd be. There's a sofa and a big chair—and the rest rooms and water to wash—"

"We figured," she said firmly, "after we got ahead some we'd send a donation to the minister. It'd only be fair."

"And?" said Donaldson. He and Stacey were feeling gratified and amused. On the floor there against the wall were a couple of cans of spray paint, a hammer and a big carving knife.

"Well, we'd just got here and settled down," said Calloway, "when we heard this noise, these two talking and laughing out here, and some dirty talk too—and I came to see what was going on, and I'll be damned if these two goddamn kids—"

"Brock."

"Well, I'm sorry, honey, but I feel like swearing, think about it. They're tearing up the Bible off the pulpit, they're saying this gonna teach all the crazy church people there isn't no God—well, I was mad," said Calloway apologetically. "I banged them around a little before I rightly saw they were just kids. But I'd do it again," he added. "Tearing up a Bible!"

The kids were sullen and defiant. "My dad finds out you beat me up, he'll kill you!" said one of them.

Stacey laughed. "And it's not a felony, but we're glad to lay our hands on these two. You know, I sort of think, Mr. Calloway, when the minister here knows about this, he'll see you and your wife have a place to stay until you get on your feet."

"We aren't asking any charity," she said quickly. "We'd pay him back, as soon as we could."

"Sure you would. Call it practical Christianity," said Stacey.

They took the two kids in. Reluctantly they parted with names. Harold Sutter, Don Hurst. Their ages and addresses.

"Now why did you want to make all the mess in the churches?" asked Donaldson.

The Hurst boy said, "They're all a lotta crap, churches. My dad says so, he's a atheist, he says it's crap about God. Besides, it was fun—it was real wild, a ball, when we done it the first time—it was Harry's idea—"

"Was not, you said—"

"It was real crazy fun—all the crap them people believe, God and Satan and angels—it was kind of a joke like, that was all—I don't care what the fuzz do to us, my dad he'll think it was a big joke too—"

"How'd you get around at night?" They were thirteen and fourteen. "Aren't you supposed to be home?"

They looked at each other and giggled. "Oh, sure," said Harold. "But Don can drive his brother's car, it's always parked just in front, and we just said we was goin' to sleep over with each other—and besides, my dad won't care either."

"It was just kind of a joke—and we're just kids, you can't do anything to kids—" How early they did learn that one.

CHAPTER 8

Maddox wanted to see Jim Mainwaring sometime today, and Paxton. But he looked at his rather cluttered desk when he came in and found Garcia's neatly typed report and read it. "Joe," he said, "you and César were on this, weren't you?—take a look." Feinman read the report and handed it on to Rodriguez. "I'll be damned," he said. "That looked like a perfectly ordinary break-in, the kind of thing that happens fifty times a week."

"Very pretty," said Rodriguez. "Oh, yes. Never underestimate the power of a woman."

"The girl who went into hysterics?" asked Feinman. "I thought she was more shook up than was natural, just finding the Edwards woman knocked out."

"The other one," said Rodriguez. "Why was the front door unlocked? We both slipped up there, Joe—if the Edwards woman had stayed after closing time for some reason, she'd have locked the door."

"I took it for granted the employees would have keys—that was how the other girl—"

"It's just a little thing," said Rodriguez. "Like all these other little things," and he grinned at the report.

"She might have had a fight with the boy friend, and he set it up—"

"Why?" asked Rodriguez. "She wouldn't be meeting a boy friend at the beauty shop. Why was it important to set it up as the ordinary break-in? So nobody would think it had been a personal fight. The door had to be unlocked so the Angela girl could walk in and give the alarm. Whatever the fight was about, it was something to do with her job, because that's where it happened. And who else was involved with the beauty shop?"

"I still say you're reaching a little, but it could be. Anyway, the Edwards woman is going to come to eventually and tell us about it."

"I wonder. I'd just," said Rodriguez, "like to find out whether my flair for detection is still working."

They left Maddox talking with D'Arcy about Mainwaring. The address in the phone book was Linwood Drive. It was a small stucco house painted pink, on a shady curving block. After Rodriguez had pushed the bell three times, May Reuther opened the door. She was wearing a woolly robe and looked sleepy and irritated. She looked at them in surprise. "Well, you're certainly up bright and early on Sunday morning. What brings you here? Don't tell me you've caught the burglar."

"No," said Rodriguez, "but a couple of queer little things have turned up that we'd like to talk to you about, Mrs. Reuther."

"Well, come in. You'll have to excuse how I look. At least let me start some coffee." They waited, in a neat and nicely furnished living room, until she came back with a tray, three mugs, a pot of coffee, cream and sugar. "Microwave oven—it's handy when you're in a hurry." She sat down opposite them and poured coffee. "Now, what's it all about?"

"We've just seen a lab report about that break-in, Mrs. Reuther." Rodriguez smiled at her. "And some funny things showed up. It looked as if the burglar broke in that back window and climbed in, and Mrs. Edwards surprised him, they had a struggle and he knocked her down, and ransacked the place for money—including her handbag—and left the same way. Or by the front door, which was unlocked."

"Yes?" she said.

"Well, it seems strange that he didn't leave any marks on the window frame or the table right beneath the window. It was a very wet night, and the alley in back would have been muddy. It's also odd that the only fingerprints on Mrs. Edwards' handbag, which was a shiny plastic one that would take prints easily, are her own. And furthermore, the window was broken from inside—we can tell, you know." She was sitting smoking quietly, eyes downcast. "Can you think of any explanation for all that?"

She didn't say anything until she'd finished her coffee, lit a new cigarette. Then she said, "I suppose you know Leila's going to be all right, and she'd tell you anyway when she can talk. I just made a mess of the whole thing. I'd better tell you about it so you won't get any wrong ideas."

"Maybe you'd better," said Feinman.

May Reuther looked at them straightly. "I'd built that shop up over twenty years, I had a regular clientele, good class. I always hired the best operators I could get, good girls, nice girls, we had a reputation for good work. There were usually three girls there besides me. But when Bill, my husband, got so bad I had to be with him, he dreaded the thought of a nursing home and I promised him he'd never go to one. It meant I had to be home all the time with him, and hire a part-time nurse. He had bone cancer, they couldn't do anything for him. And I advertised for somebody to run the shop—I hated to do it but there wasn't any other way. And Leila Edwards looked to be a pretty good bet—she'd worked at some good-class places, and she seemed to know the business end and be efficient. Where I made the mistake," she said bitterly, "was not wondering why she'd changed jobs so often. I only checked two places, Bullocks' and the Magic Comb shop, and of course they said she was a competent operator, so I gave her the job."

"And what was wrong with her?" asked Rodriguez.

May Reuther said bluntly, "She's a dyke, that's what's wrong. And she hadn't even the sense to keep it covered up, on the job. Before Bill got so bad I used to drop in when I could, and it worried me when I saw that some of my best regular clients didn't seem to be coming in— but I didn't have time to worry much, just about Bill. Only the take was falling off too. Then when Bill died—last month—I was exhausted, I wasn't up to doing anything for a while. But when I did go to the shop I found the business was right down the drain—she'd been there about six months then. About five appointments a day, and only that Angela girl there—Leila Edwards' little piece of fluff, if you get me—and a half-trained operator at that. I called some of my old regular clients, they'd all known me for years, and they all told me what had been going on. Her and the Angela girl all lovey-dovey right in the shop, it was obvious what they were, and—my God—Leila'd even tried to make up to some clients—and naturally the clients stopped coming in."

Rodriguez laughed. "You'd think she'd have better sense."

"Wouldn't you? But she didn't. It's going to take me at least a couple of years to build up the business again, if I ever can, and I was damned mad. Of course I fired her, and she said we were on a monthly basis and she'd stay to the end of the month, Angela too. Well, that wasn't long and she couldn't do much more harm. I never meant what happened," said May Reuther dispiritedly. "I'd dropped by the shop to pick up the books, I wanted to have a look at where I stood. It was just closing time and she was there alone, Angela had left early. Leila was getting ready to leave too, and somehow just the look of her standing there riled me, and I said something about Angela, never mind what, it wasn't very ladylike, and she flared up and said to keep my dirty tongue off Angie and she gave me a shove and knocked me down against the desk. And, well, I lost my temper. I hit her back, and we had a regular no-holds-barred fight all over the floor of the shop—"

Feinman said, "As simple as that."

"It didn't last long. I caught her a lucky one and she went over backwards and cracked her skull on that chair. I thought she was just knocked out, and then when she didn't come to I looked at her, and I thought she was dead. She was dead—I couldn't find any pulse—and I thought, my God, I've killed her, and what do I do now? It was all enough of a rotten mess anyway without me ending up in jail for murder."

"So you thought of faking the break-in?"

She nodded glumly. "Nobody'd know I'd been there. She hadn't marked me on the face, only a little bruise I could cover with makeup. I tried to think of everything, but I guess I didn't, I never thought about the mud in the alley, and I didn't know you could tell which side a window was broken. Her bag had got knocked off one of the little tables, things spilled out of it, and I just grabbed her wallet, and the money out of the cash box. I thought it looked kosher, and I knew you'd never pick up anybody for it." She stabbed out her cigarette. "Then when I found she wasn't dead—and the hospital says she's going to be all right—oh, God, I suppose you arrest me now."

Feinman laughed. "That'll be up to Mrs. Edwards. I can't see that you've broken any laws, you can do what you like in your own shop, can't you? If she wants to accuse you of assault, it'll be something else. But you say she started it."

She shut her eyes and leaned back, looking almost sick with relief. "I hadn't—thought of it that way," she murmured. And after a moment a little color came back to her cheeks, and she said, "I'll lay money she won't. For one thing she knows I haven't got much money, and she wouldn't find it so easy to get another job if all this came out in court and got in the papers."

Maddox and D'Arcy got to the West Hollywood apartment at nine o'clock. When the door opened to them Maddox said, "We thought we'd catch you before you went out somewhere, Mr. Mainwaring—say walking on the beach."

He stepped back in silence and they went into the living room. "We've got a few more questions for you now. We understand that you had a serious argument with your father a week ago Friday night. Would you care to tell us what it was about?"

Jim Mainwaring sat down on the couch and looked at them thoughtfully. He was just up; he wore pajamas and robe, and he hadn't shaved. "I'm rather surprised you don't already know," he said. "There's never been any secret about it. Anybody who knows me could tell you."

"About what?" asked D'Arcy.

He rummaged in the drawer of the end table, found a package of cigarettes and lit one. "So she decided to ring the gong on me, about that night. I wonder if she's got an alibi herself. That's a damn uncharitable thing to say, excuse me. The trouble between Father and me. That night was just the culmination. The end. The goddamned end of the ride on the merry-go-round." He looked at his cigarette. "She could tell you chapter and verse, as I see she already has. I suppose she heard most of it, so I might as well tell you my version. I don't know much about the police. Whether you'd understand it at all."

"You can try us and see, Mr. Mainwaring," said Maddox.

He let out a long sigh. After a dragging moment he said, "Genes are funny things. It's obvious I belong in the family somewhere, with this pronounced beak of mine"—he passed a hand over it absently—"but I seem to be a different breed from the Mainwarings like him."

"You know you were adopted?"

"After the way I found out, do you think I'd ever forget it?" He wasn't bitter, only logical. "I must have been about six, it was just before I was sent away to school. I called her Mother, and she said, I'm not your mother, some dirty little slut's your mother—she said, he wouldn't look at my son, he had to pick you out of the gutter. Of course I didn't know what she meant until later, but—"

Maddox asked him, "Did you ever ask who your parents were?"

"Once. He just said it didn't matter, my mother had been a cousin of his and I was just as much a Mainwaring as he was. That wasn't the trouble. That doesn't worry me. Why should it? I've always had to be self-sufficient. But he'd taken the trouble of adopting me and raising me, the next Mainwaring generation, to take over his beloved money and his beautiful business, and I was just no damned good to him. I'd tried to tell him, you know—since I was about sixteen and began to understand it myself. We come all shapes and sizes, with different abilities, and I've just got no head for figures. I'm no good at that kind of thing, in fact I'm damned stupid, which old Schultz—and Father— were always letting me know."

"Mr. Schultz told us you were doing fine at the job."

He barked a laugh. "My God, wouldn't he? Father dead, for all Schultz and Gower knew I'd inherit the whole shebang and be in a position to throw my weight around. Naturally they wouldn't say a word about what a dunce the son and heir is. The fact is, I'm hopeless. But he wouldn't let me go—he wouldn't let me go—he wouldn't let me go!" That was suddenly savage. He had gotten up and was standing with his back to them looking out the window. "You know, he was stupid too in some ways. So damned stupid. He just couldn't accept the fact that I was never going to learn what came so easy to him, that I didn't want to, that there's anything more important to do besides understanding money and business. We were talking different languages to each other. You see, I think maybe someday I can paint—and that's all I want to do, it's all I've ever wanted to do since I began to grow up. I don't know if I'd ever be any damn good at all—and I've never had any training—nothing—I don't know, but it's all that's important to me. How he laughed the first time I tried to tell him—asked if I could go in for the basic training—I was going through some silly idealistic phase the way all adolescents did, I'd soon get over it, it was absurd. Drawing lessons, he called it. God, I've tried, on my own—anatomy, basic color, but without any training in basic techniques, the solid groundwork— He didn't laugh later on. He tried being patient, and he tried shouting at me, and he tried reasoning with me, and he never remotely understood that nothing was going to change the nature I was born with. To him, anybody with a normal I.Q. could learn mathematics and how to operate a calculator, and he thought I was just being stubborn and uncooperative. Not applying myself, he put it. God, how I tried to explain it to him, until I saw it was simply no use. And you'll say"—he swung around, went back to the coffee table for another cigarette—"why didn't I just walk out and go my own way, be my own man?" He gave them a mirthless grin. "It isn't easy to walk out on plenty of money, when you've always had it. There's the basic training I'd need, before I could try even commercial art, drafting—before I could earn anything at that. God, God, I used to beg him, let me take something else in school, something I'm good at, can do—but it had to be solid math and science and accounting and business management—I'd have flunked out if I hadn't gotten the grades in English and languages, and I just barely made it through Stanford, with Rick's help. And you see, I thought—last year when he gave me the job in accounting, this will finally get it through to him that I'm no use, period, forever and a day, at this kind of work, and maybe he'll give up on me and let me go my own way. Hah," said Mainwaring. "I should have known him better by then."

"He didn't?" said Maddox.

"Shouting at me—and calling me names. I must be a pansy, a damn queer, wanting to draw pictures. I got mad the first time he called me that, and it was all the way downhill from then on. I hadn't talked to him except at the office for three months. I never went to the house, after I got out of college. Then"—Mainwaring drew a long breath— "Paul Andre had a show at the county museum, and Rick got me in with the press interviewer—that was a week ago Wednesday—it was a chance to meet him— Andre! One of the best men working today—I never dreamed there would be a chance he'd give me five minutes, I just hoped—God, I can't believe how lucky I was, and how he was to me—letting me talk to him when the interviewer was gone—I hadn't dared to hope he'd even be willing to look, but I'd brought a couple of small canvases, and—he did. He said—he said to me, I think you have the root of the matter in you, young man—you are untutored, you know nothing, but there is an eye for line and color—Andre said that to me!" His tone was nearly reverent. "And he said he'd speak for a place for me at the Wyndham Institute. Wyndham! You wouldn't know, but about the best training to be had, the Wyndham in New York. The tuition's high and they only take so many students— God, to think of the chance!" Mainwaring was silent, and then said with a little laugh, "So I made one last try. I went to see him that night."

"And it turned into a fight?" asked D'Arcy.

"The last one." He gave them a crooked smile. "I tried to spell it out in simple words, appeal to his reason. He could see I was hopeless at what he wanted me to do, wouldn't it be better to find out if I wasn't so stupid at what I wanted to do? But what I wanted to do was just footling foolishness to him, and he blew up at me. But good. For the last time. He'd spent a fortune bringing me up and educating me, and I was a damned half-wit with no sense of responsibility or principle—the only damn fool idea in my head to waste time drawing pictures—and he was through with me, he'd come to the end of his patience. I was no damned good, and he was going to cut me out of his will—I could try to use some common sense and do some useful work at the job, or Schultz could fire me and I could go to hell my own way, maybe if I had to earn my own keep I'd grow up and turn into a man. Kaput. Finis."

"I see," said Maddox. "And what then?"

"I got out. What else? I sat up thinking all night, but there was no way out. I'd thought, if he would go for the tuition and a reasonable allowance—it'd have been nothing to him— But I'm not qualified for any job, which was his fault, God knows—and even if I could get a job

I could handle back there, I couldn't afford the tuition." He was silent a long while, and then he said in an almost indifferent tone, "But oddly enough, I didn't murder him. I got it all off my chest to Rick the next night, and I really did go to that movie, and came home and went to bed. And I've never owned a gun. But there's no way I can prove it to you, of course."

The sergeant Feinman had talked to in Glassboro called back about noon. "Say, we can't find a smell of this Hinman at any of the hotels or motels around. He could be staying with relatives, but if so it's a different name." Feinman passed on the temporary plate number. "That might be a help. It could be, if he's decided to stay in Jersey, he's already applied to the D.M.V. for registration. But, a funny thing —the coincidences, they do come along. I was talking to the chief about this yesterday, and he was interested, the body under the house, and he said the very first case he worked on as a detective was a body under a house. Right here, twenty-two years ago, how about that?"

Feinman felt a little cold draft up the back of his neck. "Coincidences are funny all right."

"Well, we'll have another look with this new information, and let you know."

Feinman intended to call Warrensburg and the other towns to pass on the plate number, and rather to his own surprise he found himself asking the sergeant in Warrensburg, "You ever had a homicide with a body buried under a house?"

The sergeant laughed and said, "Not in my time anyway."

Maddox and D'Arcy came back, and Rodriguez had left Franks' report on Maddox's desk. He looked at it and said, "That must have been one hell of a job. Pontiacs, and only to three years back." He handed it on to D'Arcy, who asked where it could send them. "That hit-run was at the corner of Yucca and Whitley. That's all old residential up there, and not on the way to anywhere. Of course the driver might have been visiting an old aunt and maybe he lives in San Francisco and he'll never be in five hundred miles of the area again. But it's just worth a cast. Brief the watch commander in Traffic to tell the beat men covering that area to keep an eye out for a royal-blue Pontiac parked anywhere up there."

D'Arcy said, "Worth a try. There may still be evidence on the car." He went out to the Traffic office. The autopsy report on that O.D. was in, the body hadn't been identified yet. D'Arcy came back and Maddox gave Feinman and Rodriguez the rundown on Jim Mainwaring. "And what ideas do we come up with now?" asked D'Arcy. "God knows, he probably felt he had the motive, but—"

"I've always understood," said Maddox, "that one of the strongest forces in human nature is the creative urge. That poor young devil was caught between a rock and a hard place. No way out, as he said." He leaned back in the desk chair and watched the smoke from his cigarette wafting in spirals toward the ceiling. "Have you ever heard how Stephen Foster died?"

Rodriguez looked at him curiously. "Is it relevant?"

Maddox said vaguely, "I was just thinking, that wasn't a very happy house or family, damn all the money. I came across the story on Foster in something I was reading once. All his songs, part of our history, aren't they?—people still singing them. He wasn't a very practical man. He had tuberculosis and sometimes he drank too much, and he never had much money. When a friend found him dying, and got him into a charity hospital, the friend had to hunt all through the morgue to find his body, to give him some sort of funeral. He was only thirty-eight. And all he had on him when he died was an old purse with seventy cents in change and a piece of paper with an idea for a song scribbled on it—*dear friends and gentle hearts.*"

Feinman rubbed his jaw. "Yes, it doesn't really matter a damn what a man has, the important thing is what he is. Nobody's going to remember Charles Mainwaring in a hundred years."

"Him and his family tree. Yes, Jim Mainwaring had a very concrete motive, didn't he? He was going to be worse off, when Mainwaring made that new will. That's what Mainwaring was doing just before he died, starting to draft a new will for Sanford. And who knows how he'd have treated his wife? If he suspected her of being involved with Paxton? One thing I do know, for whatever reason she went down to the study that night, it wasn't to tell Charles not to sit up late. She thought Jim had killed him, and she couldn't care less, she says. That rang true, anyway."

D'Arcy said, "The son had one hell of a lot stronger motive. She hasn't any really."

"Yes, but both of them hated the man and I think she'd be the stronger hater. Would it do any good," said Maddox dreamily, "to go up there and have a thorough hunt all around that yard, under all those old bushes and hedges, for the gun?"

"After a week?" asked D'Arcy.

"Think about it. If she shot him, and if she was alone there as she claims, what would she do with the gun? If she knew it couldn't be traced to anybody, leave it there and hope it got written off as suicide. So the gun was registered, and she didn't dare. It could have belonged to Paxton. She wouldn't care if it could be traced to Jim, or would she? I don't think so. She knows the maid is in, would hear her drive a car out. She can surmise that the police will be searching the house. If she'd thought straight, she'd have copied Mrs. Reuther's simple little idea and faked a break-in, but in any case she had to get rid of the gun. What else could she do but go out and shove it well out of sight under one of those hedges? I don't think she'd have risked showing enough light to bury it."

"And she's had time to retrieve it," said Feinman.

"Has she? Would she? It's been raining most of the week, and she's had people in and out of the house—and the maid there all day and night. Has she had the chance? And she'll be thinking, if we haven't gone hunting by now we won't, may as well leave it."

"Possible," said D'Arcy.

"If it was Jim—yes, that film about Gauguin, another unrecognized painter—he could have had the gun, and got so stirred up over the movie that he went home and got it. And realized we could trace it to him. Another thing we'd better do, just as busywork, is to find out if any of them ever had a gun registered. D'Arcy, you can start the machinery on that with R. and I. downtown. If it was Jim, he threw it off the pier at the beach and will tell us it was stolen. But I think we'll have a look for the gun because the only reason it was taken away was that it can be traced, and if we can find it that might give us a clearer idea who fired it. Though"—he sat up and laughed—"they can be very easily acquired sometimes. Look at Roy Kelsey."

The last couple of days the press had been devoting a lot of space to Roy Kelsey. That would die down by tomorrow. Kelsey would be, they could guess, charged with second-degree homicide and probably arraigned sometime next week.

Two more heists went down on Sunday night, but the witnesses couldn't give a description on one, and the other one was the fellow in the ski mask again, or another one with the same idea. They liked to think this was a good well-trained force, but nobody could make bricks without straw, and a lot of crimes happened that went unsolved. It was one of the facts of life.

Monday was D'Arcy's day off. The day men had hardly gotten in when a new homicide was called in, and Rodriguez went out resignedly to look at it.

It turned out to be a suicide, an old woman of eighty-four who had lived in a little three-room apartment built over a garage. There wasn't any note, but the woman who owned the property and lived in the front house, and had found her, could tell him all about it.

"Poor old Mrs. Cannon," she said. "She said that to me when she moved in here ten years ago—after her husband died—I didn't quite believe her, I said you wouldn't do a thing like that—and she said she and her husband had agreed, whichever one was left alone, when they got too old to take care of themselves and in bad health, the only sensible thing to do was take a peaceful way out. And he was a pharmacist and he'd gotten some kind of poison or sleeping tablets, I don't know what, all put away to use. She hadn't been feeling well lately, and she hadn't much money, but I never thought she'd really do it. Poor old Mrs. Cannon."

Rodriguez went back to the station to write the report, and found Feinman alone in the office, sitting bolt upright with one hand on the telephone, staring at the opposite wall and looking as if he'd seen a ghost.

"What's struck you?" asked Rodriguez, sitting down and rummaging in the left drawer for report forms.

Feinman licked his lips. "I just had a phone call," he said. "From that sergeant in Warrensburg."

"Have they picked up Hinman?"

"No," said Feinman. "No. Not yet. When I was talking to him yesterday I happened to ask him—I really don't know why—if they'd ever had a case of a body buried under a house. He'd never heard of one. But he called me back just now—I guess he took me literally—to say he'd asked around, and the oldest detective on the force, Sergeant Nunn, said yes, they'd had a case like that about sixteen years back."

Rodriguez was mildly interested. "You don't say. The long arm of coincidence."

"It was," said Feinman, "a house on the outskirts of town, and the owner had been renting it out. When he decided to move back into it he was doing some renovating, and the body turned up under the floor of a closet. The doctor said it was a woman, and she'd probably been dead three or four years. During that period of time there'd been three or four people renting the house, and a couple of them had moved out of town. They never did identify the body or find out anything more about it."

Rodriguez put the report forms down and turned to look at him.

"What I didn't mention," said Feinman, "is that that sergeant in Glassboro, when he called back, was talking about coincidences too. They'd had a case like that there. A body under a house. He didn't go into details, but it was twenty-two years ago."

"¡Santa Maria!" said Rodriguez. "What the hell is in your mind, Joe?"

"Hinman was living there in Glassboro up to twenty-six years ago. It probably didn't get found right away, that body. He was living in Warrensburg up to nineteen years ago. And there were two of them under the house on Ardmore, one older than the other." They looked at each other in silence.

"Now really," said Rodriguez. "Really."

"Well, it seems—queer," said Feinman. "Just a little too much coincidence involved. Or am I just overimaginative?"

Rodriguez opened his mouth and shut it. Feinman's phone rang again and he looked reluctant to pick it up, but did. "Yes, this is Feinman." It was the manager of a Bank of America in Hollywood.

"I'm glad to tell you that we have finally located that account for you. The Hinman account. It's been inactive for some time, and it was closed out just recently. There was a savings account of five thousand dollars—"

"Where was it transferred?"

"To a state bank in Corinth, New York. Mr. Hinman took a thousand in cash, and the rest—"

"Yes, thanks very much," said Feinman automatically. Rodriguez had rolled the report forms into his typewriter, but hadn't started to type yet. "Four coincidences," said Feinman.

"They do happen. It's a big country."

There was a little silence. "Maddox wants everybody out to help on that hunt. Eleven o'clock," said Rodriguez. He started to type the report.

Three minutes later Feinman, who had gone on staring into space, said, "I wonder about Glens Falls and Corinth."

"Look," said Rodriguez, "we've helped considerably to shoot up the L.A.P.D.'s phone bill this month. We've got enough business on hand as it is."

"You don't like it any better than I do," said Feinman.

"I've got an imagination, which I try to curb," said Rodriguez. He finished the report, rolled the forms out of the typewriter and separated them neatly. Then he sat there looking at them without signing them. "Sixteen years ago in Warrensburg?"

"And the doctor said she'd been dead three or four years, which would make it the year Hinman moved away or the year before."

"Yes," said Rodriguez.

"It just seems—"

"Oh, it's got to be coincidence," said Rodriguez.

"It wouldn't do any harm to call Glens Falls and Corinth."

"We've got to turn out on that search. When we have time—there can't be one damn thing to it," said Rodriguez firmly.

George Ellis was feeling unreasonably annoyed at Maddox. He had stripped the office of every man for that damn-fool search for that gun, and somebody had to mind the store. Ellis had some paperwork to do, and it seemed that no sooner was the office empty than things started happening.

Traffic called in a rumor that a gang rumble was arranged for a junior-high campus this afternoon. And only Ralston manning the Juvenile bureau, thought Ellis. Damn. He was just starting out for lunch when two new burglaries were reported within five minutes of each other. At least he had a few lab men to send out.

He had just gotten back from lunch when another call came in, and he used a few cusswords he hadn't come out with in months. And when he got there, it was a goddamned mess.

About one o'clock a jumper had gone off the top of a medical building on Melrose, and by disastrous chance had landed squarely on top of a man walking innocently along the sidewalk. It made quite a little work for a street-cleaning truck after the morgue wagon had gotten there, and a couple of women had fainted. Ellis had to go down to the morgue to get identification, if possible.

The jumper's wallet was intact; there wasn't much in it but a driver's license for Robert Farrell, a few bills, but among those was a little slip, reminder of office appointment with Dr. Werner. The address was the medical building. The innocent bystander had been identified at the scene by one of the fainting women, who was his sister. He was Julian Peterson, and he'd just gotten to town from Wichita, Kansas, for a vacation.

Ellis went to see Dr. Werner in the medical building. He was a psychiatrist, and he was very surprised to hear about Farrell, who had left his office about ten minutes before he jumped. "He's been a little depressed, but I certainly didn't consider him suicidal, or I'd have taken steps to restrain him. This really does astonish me, Lieutenant."

It had, thought Ellis, astonished Mr. Peterson even more.

On the grounds of the Mainwaring house, all of them were swearing at Maddox for having this brainwave. From all the recent rain, the ground was soggy and muddy, especially where they were looking deep under bushes. The house was an old one, and the landscaping was thick. They groveled about, groping and using flashlights, and getting their clothes dirty, and of course they didn't find a thing. The maid was watching from an upstairs window.

Rodriguez and Feinman were not thinking much about this particular murder. Nobody but Maddox had expected to find a gun, and they didn't. When they knocked off at four-thirty, Maddox, who was as muddy as the rest of them, lit a cigarette with a dirty hand and said, "Paxton. That's the other obvious answer. She phoned Paxton and he got rid of the gun for her."

"So we'll never lay eyes on it," said Rodriguez. "We'll never pin this one on anybody—there's just not enough evidence on it. Solid evidence for a judge and jury to look at."

"Damn it," said Maddox, "I don't know why we should get hot and bothered about it, César. Force of habit, I suppose—automatically try to solve any case that shows up. The man was something of a bastard, and I'm sorry for the son, if I don't think much of Avis."

"And there's something new I think you'd better hear about," said Rodriguez.

"Well, before we do anything else," said Maddox, "let's go back to the station and get some of this mud off."

When they were reasonably clean again, they foregathered in the office and Feinman started to say, "César thinks I'm coming down with brain fever, or says so, but I think you ought to hear about it. It's in outer space, and I know coincidences do happen, but—"

"I'll admit to you," said Rodriguez, "I think it's just a little funny too. Maybe just a little."

Maddox was listening inattentively. There was a report in a manila envelope on his desk, from R. and I. downtown; he extracted it and scanned it rapidly. "So we might guess at part of the truth," he said sardonically, "if we never get the solid evidence to pin it down legally. Since about four years ago, Joel Paxton has owned a .22 Hi-Standard revolver. Does anybody want to guess what he's going to tell us about it?"

"That it was stolen from his office," said Nolan and Dowling together.

Maddox looked at his watch. "It's too late to catch him now. Tomorrow. But—"

"Yes," said Nolan thoughtfully, "but it's a common gun, Sergeant. A lot of them around."

"Unfortunately true," said Maddox, "but it's suggestive, isn't it? Oh, hell, we've all had a day and it's nearly quitting time. You can pass on your new idea in the morning, Joe."

The gusty wind had gone away and it was again gray and overcast. As Rodriguez turned out of the parking lot he snapped on the car radio, to a local news station. He debated whether to go home and put a TV dinner in the oven or save trouble by going out for dinner.

"—in the L.A. area," said the radio, coming on suddenly. "After an unusual early storm center hit the city last week, more rain is predicted in the next few days. And now to the local news—"

"*Condenación*," said Rodriguez, who felt somewhat like a cat about rain.

"—and it is expected that Kelsey will be arraigned on Thursday or Friday of the coming week. The district attorney's office had no official comment."

Rodriguez turned onto Western. His apartment was up on Los Feliz. He caught the light at Franklin, and sat somnolently watching it.

"And also on the local scene, a strange discovery was made today at the duplex home of Mr. Frederick Fenton of Long Beach. Employees of an extermination service, routinely inspecting the building for termites, had occasion to remove the floorboard of a closet, and discovered a partly decomposed body. Mr. Fenton, who lives in the second unit of the duplex, has stated—"

"*¡Jesu, Maria y Josef!*" said Rodriguez.

When the new Traffic shift got briefed, Johnny McCrea was told about that royal-blue Pontiac to watch for. Possibly the one on that hit-run. All too vividly McCrea remembered that poor little girl, the crushed body thrown against the curb, and the two weeping women. He didn't have any idea how the front-office boys had pinpointed the car, but his not to reason why.

As he cruised his route, whenever he wandered up north of Hollywood Boulevard, dutifully he kept an eye out for Pontiacs. He didn't really expect to see the right car, and he was more surprised than any-thing else when he did. It was after his Code Seven break that he took a swing north on Highland, turned up Yucca and went along some of the side streets up there. As he turned a corner the squad's lights caught a car parked in the driveway of the corner house, and it was a Pontiac. It looked nearly new.

He couldn't be sure of the color at night. He left the squad idling and walked a few feet up the drive with his flashlight; the corner streetlight helped. The Pontiac was about a year old, and it was royal blue. Just to be thorough about it, he took the plate number, went back to the squad and called it in. The Pontiac was registered to Bertram J. Crosby of this address, which was on Grace Street. There were no wants or warrants on it.

McCrea entered it into his notebook. He wondered if that was the car that had killed the little girl. Well, the front-office boys could take it from here.

CHAPTER 9

Maddox had just gotten home when Rodriguez called him. "Both Joe and I had a little uneasy feeling about it, but it seemed far out, and then on my way home the local news station—" Maddox was incredulous.

"But, my God, if it's the same Fenton—"

"It's got to be."

"Yes, if it is we'd better find out about this from Long Beach, and add in what we've got. But of all the impossible things—"

Rodriguez said dryly, "And call Glens Falls and Corinth."

"What? Oh, I see what you mean. But—my God, leaping to conclusions—"

"Don't drag your feet," said Rodriguez.

He told Sue and Margaret about it over dinner, and they were equally incredulous. "It's out of an implausible mystery thriller," said Sue.

But when they talked to the Long Beach detective, Sergeant Fuller, who was handling the case, the next morning, it appeared that there was some solid evidence to look at. Maddox and Rodriguez got down there by nine o'clock, and Fuller, who was probably nearing retirement, stout and bald, but with a mind as sharp as it ever had been, filled them in.

"Fenton nearly passed out," he said. "He was going to have the place painted, and the painter said he'd better have a termite inspection first, and they found termites and took up part of the closet floor to see how bad it was, and there was the body."

"Have you got anything from the doctors yet?" asked Rodriguez.

"No, but Fenton recognized a pin."

"A pin?"

"Lady's brooch," said Fuller, and took a plastic evidence bag from the top desk drawer and upended it on the desk. "It's just costume stuff, and there's nothing to get from it, no prints. Fenton said he remembered seeing Mrs. Hinman wearing it." It was tarnished and

dull, jewelers' brass, made in the shape of a little cat. "Listen," said
Fuller, "this rigmarole you started to tell me—for God's sake, we do
automatically tend to look at a husband or wife, the other one gets
murdered. And why hide the body if it wasn't murder? There's nothing
to say what killed her, if this is Hinman's wife. But what you're saying
about Hinman—God almighty, you think he murdered these other
women too?"

"Well, look at the score," said Maddox. "We were damned lucky to
identify the Parfitt woman, and that gives us a date. We know he was
living at the house on Ardmore when she disappeared, probably when
she was killed. We haven't got many details on the cases back east yet,
but you can see how it would be—how we know it went in the house in
Warrensburg—the same way it went here. When the body turned up, it
wasn't possible to pin down even the year the woman died, and in the
possible time span there were several different tenants occupying the
house. The police didn't find all of them to talk to. But if there are any
old records to look at, I'll lay you any money that we're going to find
Hinman was one of the tenants."

"I wonder," said Rodriguez, "if Joe's got anything from Glens Falls
and Corinth yet." He called up to Hollywood, and Feinman said, his
voice sounding rather hollow, that Glens Falls had had one. "Eight
years ago. A block of old houses had been getting knocked down
where a new shopping center was going in, and the bulldozer turned up
a skeleton. They didn't bother to figure out exactly which house it had
been under, or where—all they did was bury it. The doctor said it was
female, no telling how long it had been buried. Most of the houses had
been vacant for a long time. Corinth says they never had such a case."

"Yes?" said Rodriguez. "I wonder where he lived in Corinth. If they
went there and took up the floorboards in a closet—"

"My God, César, this is beyond a joke."

"I wasn't joking," said Rodriguez. He relayed that to Maddox and
Fuller.

"It's so wild it's almost funny," said Maddox. "And you know where
this is going to take us, don't you? It's no joke, César—Corinth indeed
had better have a look at where Hinman lived there. And where did
you find out he'd lived around here? My God, how to get the addresses
—but I'm a fool, of course the personnel office at Lester's will have all
that, or would they?"

"I should think so," said Rodriguez. "We'll ask. But, my good God,
he couldn't have left one every place he'd lived, could he? If it's a joke
it's a damned bad one."

"You know we'll have to look, just to be sure. At least we'll know where to look, if and when we get the addresses. It seems to be his favorite spot, under the closet floor."

Fuller said, "Outer space. You can say. He must be way across the line, if this is so."

Maddox said soberly, "Well, there was Rose Parfitt's ten thousand dollars. I don't think Hinman's insane at all, I think he's a very practical man."

"And where is he?" asked Rodriguez. "He seems to have vanished into thin air."

"Well, we'd better get on with the job of backtracking him, God knows there'll be enough to do."

Feinman had already called Stanley in Lester's personnel office, and Stanley, a little puzzled at all this extraordinary interest in one of their longtime employees, had agreed to look up all those old addresses for them. It might, he said, take a little while. "And," said Feinman, "while you were gone I had a phone call from a lawyer. A Sylvester Endicott, which sounds nearly too good, doesn't it? He's representing Mrs. Mainwaring, and he's advised her to give us a new statement in his presence, and he'll bring her in tomorrow afternoon if that's convenient to us."

"The hell you say," said Maddox. "I wonder what she'll say this time. Well, it may be this afternoon before we hear from Stanley. Has anything new gone down?"

"Knifing at a junior high. D'Arcy's on it. Thank God that gang fight didn't materialize—of course it may yet, today or tomorrow."

Maddox found a report on his desk sent up from Traffic and said, looking at it, "Well, well. Just now and then we get lucky. If this is the right car. The time, the place and the loved one all together— One of the squads spotted a royal-blue Pontiac on Grace Street." He got out the county guide and looked it up. "Just around the corner and a few blocks from Yucca and Whitley, isn't that nice. Mr. Bertram J. Crosby. Just to fill in the time, I think I'd like to talk to Mr. Crosby." He drove up there, to a comfortable old bungalow on a corner. A woman answered the door, and Maddox showed her the badge. "Mrs. Crosby?" She was about forty, not bad-looking, ready to go out somewhere, by the coat and the handbag in one hand.

"Yes?" She didn't look alarmed, only curious.

"We're looking for your husband, if that's Bertram Crosby. We think he can give us some information."

"Well, he's at his office, of course. He has a tax-service business," and she gave him the address, far down on Western.

It was a double storefront, and looked to be a fairly prosperous concern: almost any tax accountant would be doing all right these days. He parked and walked back. There was a blond girl at a desk in a tiny anteroom. She was frightened by the badge, scurried away, scurried back to say Mr. Crosby would see him.

Crosby was a lean dark man in his forties, with deep lines like scars etched on his cheeks. When Maddox came into his small office, behind a larger open office with desks in two rows, he didn't stand up or speak. His desk was cluttered with papers, an overflowing ashtray. After a moment he said abruptly, "Christy said you're police."

"That's right." Maddox showed him the badge. "It's about your car, Mr. Crosby. The royal-blue Pontiac. We think it may have been the car involved in a hit-run accident a little over a week ago." Crosby didn't say anything. "You know, our laboratory technicians can do a lot of interesting things these days, and if it was your car they can probably turn up some evidence on it—besides what we've got. Could you tell me where your car was that night—a week ago last Friday night, about nine-thirty?"

Crosby was still silent. He put out his cigarette and instantly lit another. He swiveled his chair around to look out the window at an uninteresting view of the city. Presently he said quietly, "Hell. Maybe it's just as well, though I'm damned if I know how the police found out. I'll have nightmares about it the rest of my life. And I never did anything against the law before. If you hadn't found out about it, I'd have kept quiet and lived with it, but now—" He swiveled back and put an elbow on the desk and leaned his head in that hand.

"How did it happen?" asked Maddox coldly.

Crosby said heavily, "I'd been worried about money—well, who isn't —and I'd had two men off with flu, with the end of the year coming up there was a little workload. I'd stayed on past closing that night, I didn't get home until about nine, and just as I pulled into the drive I remembered I was out of cigarettes. I don't excuse myself—but I was damn tired, and worried, and I wanted to get in and relax. I cussed, and backed out again, and started down to the nearest place on Highland. I was going too damned fast, because I was in a hurry to get home. When I came around that corner, the lights hit her, but I couldn't have stopped to save—" He bit that off. "I was doing about forty. Just a kid—I can still feel the lurch when I hit—"

"It's a heavy car."

"My God, I must have been a little crazy—it was just, on top of everything else—I was sorry, I was sorry, but what it would cost, the trouble there'd be—I didn't stop, I went on down and stopped at a bar for a drink and cigarettes, and I thought about putting in an anonymous call but—" He put a hand to his head. "I'm sorry," he said numbly. "I suppose you're going to take me in to jail."

"You can get bail, Mr. Crosby."

"Yes, I know," he said. "I know that."

Stanley didn't get back to them until the middle of the afternoon. He read off a string of addresses to Rodriguez, the address in Corinth, Glens Falls, the addresses here—Pasadena, Monterey Park, Covina. "My God," said D'Arcy, looking at the list, "I still can't get over this damned thing, it's too much. What time is it in New York?—six-thirty. I suppose the Corinth force runs a night shift?"

Rodriguez shrugged. "Who knows? There's no hurry, D'Arcy—if there's anything there for them to find, it'll keep."

"And what a piece of news to break from three thousand miles away —excuse me, gents, you'd better drop everything else and go look under this house and you may find a surprise waiting. My God. This is the wildest one we've ever had."

"And have you thought about something else?" said Feinman. "Probably all of these places are now peacefully occupied by ordinary respectable citizens, and we'll have to get search warrants, and the citizens are going to have seven fits when we come invading their privacy, even before we start to take the floorboards up."

"Oh, it had occurred to me," said Rodriguez. "It had. Does anybody want to call Corinth, or shall we leave it till tomorrow?"

Maddox was at the other end of the room telling the tale to Nolan and Dowling, who'd been out on a burglary; they were both looking stunned and fascinated.

"We'd better talk to the people here first," said Feinman. "There'll be the warrants to get, and the sooner we get on that—and, my God, the boys back east had better go all out looking for him. Where the hell has he gone, and why, anyway? And why all of a sudden?"

"Another thought I had, Joe," said Rodriguez, "we may never know. Maybe he has found out he has an incurable disease, and went back there to revisit the scenes of his youth, and then walked into the woods and shot himself, and he'll be found as a moldering skeleton ten years from now. Or he swam out to sea and the sharks got him."

D'Arcy said vigorously, "Well, he didn't take that new Chevy with him, if he did. Somebody ought to spot that eventually."

They spent the rest of the day talking to the police in those other towns, and when the night shift would be on Maddox called Brougham, who ran out of astonished expletives before he heard all of it.

Brougham, Stacey and Donaldson were still talking about Hinman when a call came in, and Stacey and Brougham went out on it. The squad car was in the first aisle of a public parking lot on Beverly, and the uniformed man and a civilian were standing guard over another man wearing handcuffs. "Where's the ambulance?" asked the Traffic man. "I don't think she's seriously hurt, but she's still unconscious, and I called the damn ambulance before I called you—" There was a woman lying facedown on the blacktop, just behind them. The ambulance came a minute later and took her off, and the civilian said, "The damndest thing I ever saw." He was a large young man with shoulders like a football player. "I'm just getting in my car, and this couple are walking across the lot past me, all of a sudden this guy takes something out of his pocket—that wrench it was—and starts hitting the girl on the head. So I yelled and pulled him off her and belted him one, and then I spot the squad car going past so I ran out and flagged it. Damndest thing. He doesn't seem to be drunk."

The man in handcuffs was smaller and older; he just stood there looking despondent. Brougham asked, "What's your name?" He didn't answer right away and Stacey repeated the question.

He said, "My name's Charles Dickens."

"Oh, for God's sake," said Brougham. "A nut."

"No, that's my name. And I tried to tell that other cop—I told him how I killed that woman, all that time back—I don't know why he wouldn't arrest me. I told him how I keep wanting to hit women on the head, maybe there's something wrong with me. I didn't have no reason to put that wrench in my pocket tonight, and I don't know that woman, I just picked her up in the bar down the block, and I don't know why I hit her."

"Oh, for *God's* sake," said Brougham.

They took him up to the jail and booked him in, and by the I.D. on him his name really was Charles Dickens. At the station, Stacey called the emergency ward. The woman had had a wallet in her coat pocket, with I.D. in it, so they got her name for the report.

Brougham said darkly, "There are too damn many peculiar things going on around here lately."

There was a long conference in the Hollywood station on Wednesday morning, with men from Pasadena, Monterey Park and Covina. They talked it over and decided how to handle it generally. There wouldn't be any trouble about getting the warrants; they could specify exactly what they expected to find. The trouble was going to be from the householders, screaming about invasion of privacy.

"Though I will say one thing," said a scholarly-looking black sergeant from Pasadena. "When we tell them what we're looking for they may be just as glad we came, to take it away."

They dispersed to start the machinery on the warrants, and Maddox went looking for Sue. She had just gotten back from somewhere and said if he had the time and inclination he could take her to lunch, she was starving.

"I don't know that this is so good for you," said Maddox, "the rat race. Running all around. Where've you been?"

"At Juvenile Court, at the hearing on the Fogel girl. Of course they've taken custody"—she was looking worried—"and I know it's all we can do, all the court can do, but it's a dismal solution at best, isn't it? Hardly a homelike atmosphere, if she *is* safe from the lecherous papa, but—oh, damn. What else do we do about it? He's coming up for arraignment on Friday, and the other judge sent him for psychiatric evaluation, which is just a waste of time."

"Well, put your coat back on and I'll take you to lunch."

Over sandwiches and coffee he told her, "The Mainwaring woman's coming in to make a statement. Complete with lawyer. I want you to sit in on it—I'd like a female opinion of her. In fact, I may let you take the statement. See what you make of her."

"Well, all right," said Sue. She added, "I don't think the son did it. Just from what you told me."

"Why not?"

"I don't know," she said vaguely. "Just a feeling."

"There, that's what I mean. Women get feelings. Sometimes they hit the target nearer than the feelings we get. I'd like to know what feelings you get about her."

"Don't go by them," said Sue, wrinkling her nose at him. "What I know about her, I don't like. Not because she's maybe been committing adultery with somebody—"

"Oh, really," said Maddox.

"—because if she really loved the man it wouldn't matter, and I don't think it mattered to her husband. But because of what you said, the way she behaved to the little boy. That was just unforgivable, wasn't it?"

Maddox regarded her across the table seriously. "You're getting into practice for maternity."

"Don't be utterly stupid, Ivor. Any woman would feel the same way. Or most."

The lawyer Endicott brought Avis Mainwaring in about two-thirty, hovering over her protectively to let everybody know her rights were being looked after. He was a big florid man, too well-dressed, with cynical eyes, and he did the talking. He thought it advisable for Mrs. Mainwaring to make a final statement to the police, and they were clearly to understand that this was all the information she could give them. She stood silent beside him, passive, smartly dressed as usual. The funeral had been on Monday, in the Hollywood Hills section of Forest Lawn, but she was still wearing black.

Maddox took them across the hall to the little office, where Daisy discreetly removed herself. He said cheerfully, "We're a little busy here at the moment, I'm going to let Mrs. Maddox take down what you have to tell us." He left them to Sue.

They sat down, and Avis Mainwaring looked at Sue with faint curiosity. "Is he your husband?"

"That's right."

"It must be—funny—to be working together. This kind of job." She looked around the office, with its air of bare efficiency, and shrugged out of her coat before the courtly Endicott could help her.

Sue had her notebook out ready. She was covertly gauging the probable price of that coat—Magnin's, she decided—and also of the deceptively plain black sheath, the sheer nylons, the stilt-heeled black pumps. She noticed the faint lines around the eyes, the tight droop to the mouth, and she thought, I wonder how much she has to work to keep that figure, and, she probably ought to wear glasses.

"Now you needn't be nervous, my dear," said Endicott soothingly. "Just tell the whole truth, exactly as I advised you to. If some of it is a little, ah, embarrassing, that can't be helped—the important thing is that the police should have the truth."

"Yes," she said evenly. "I understand that." She had obviously been rehearsed. She went on to deliver the statement in a deliberately flat tone, with little expression.

"On the night my husband was killed, I had gone to the Ellingers'

house for dinner, just as I said before. Mr. Paxton called for me, but
my husband did not come out of his study to greet him—they were not
good friends. Mr. and Mrs. Bell were at the dinner party too, and
about nine-thirty we all went to Angelo's club in Beverly Hills. But
neither Mr. Paxton nor I cared to dance, and we left. We went—" She
paused for half a second, and went on slowly, "We went to his apartment. I have been Mr. Paxton's mistress for about a year. We stayed
there until about one-thirty in the morning, and then Mr. Paxton drove
me home."

"Is this too fast for you, Mrs. Maddox?" asked Endicott courteously.

"No, I'm getting it."

"Then go on, my dear. You're doing just fine."

"I had been thinking of divorcing my husband for some time. Mr.
Paxton and I had been discussing it—that night, that is. When I came
into the house I saw that the study light was still on, that my husband
was still up. He often sat up late reading. I decided that I would tell
him immediately that I was going to divorce him. Mr. Paxton had said
I wasn't to discuss any terms with him, it was better to leave all that—
the arrangement for a settlement—to a lawyer."

"*Quite* right," murmured Endicott.

"But I decided to tell him—and have it over with. But when I went
into the study, I found he was dead. I felt his wrist to be sure there
wasn't a pulse. But he was dead. I was frightened. I telephoned Mr.
Paxton, when I knew he had had time to get home, and asked him
what to do. By then I had seen that Charles had been shot, and that
there wasn't a gun in the room." She took a breath.

"Yes," said Sue, getting that down in her neat shorthand.

"Mr. Paxton told me—to sit tight—and not do anything. I told him
that I thought Jim had probably done it. I said that because Jim—our
adopted son—had had a violent argument with his father the previous
night. Mr. Paxton said it would be—would be one hell of a legal mess
if Jim were arrested—if most of the money was left to him—something
about not profiting by a crime. I didn't understand that. He said—the
longer we gave the damned young fool to arrange an alibi, the better—
and I should wait and let the maid find the body in the morning, and
say I'd gone straight to bed. He said he would contact the Ellingers and
the Bells and warn them to say we had all been together all evening.
They all knew about us, and would do that. Say that. Because—he said
—with the police around, they might have some wrong ideas—if they
knew about that. About motives, I mean, wrong ideas about that. So I
went up to bed the way he told me. And waited. And the maid found

Charles in the morning. I don't know anything about the murder, who killed him or why. That really is all."

"That's just fine, my dear," said Endicott. "You see, it wasn't difficult at all."

She leaned back in the straight chair and shut her eyes. Sue said, "If you'd like to wait a few minutes until I have this typed, you can sign it now, Mrs. Mainwaring."

"Yes. All right."

Endicott, eying his client in a paternal way, said, "Perhaps—a cup of coffee while we wait—"

"There's a machine at the end of the hall," said Sue. "I'm afraid only paper cups."

"No matter." He went out.

Sue rolled the carbon sheets into the typewriter, and without planning to speak at all she heard herself say, "You hated him quite a lot, didn't you?"

She had not moved from her suddenly relaxed position, perhaps from sheer relief at getting all that out. She opened her eyes and looked at Sue, and her mouth twisted in a little bitter smile. "Just between us girls?" she said. "I expect you're in love with your husband—it must be a funny feeling. Yes, I hated Charles, I'd hated him for a long time, but I stayed with him because of the money. Do you know when I started to hate him? It was after I had the baby. The poor little baby without any mind. The doctor said it was just bad luck, and there was no reason I couldn't go on and have a perfect baby—but Charles wouldn't. He said, do you think I'd take the chance of you producing another monster? But he had to have a son, to carry on his precious Mainwaring line, so do you know what he did? He found some mercenary little slut who'd have his baby, if he paid her for it. What do they call it, a surrogate mother? If I'd had children, everything might have been different—but he wouldn't let me. He never came near me again. And now he's dead, I only get half a million—half a million! And all the rest to that stupid boy. My God, he was worth ten times as much to me alive! And Joel backing off, he'll never marry me now that's all I'll get." She stopped abruptly, sitting up to fumble for a cigarette with shaking hands; and Endicott came back with the coffee.

The search warrants came through on Thursday, and various men started out to execute them, armed with an assortment of hastily assembled tools, chisels and claw hammers.

The first report came into the Hollywood station just before noon, from the Pasadena sergeant. He said to Maddox, "Bingo. Just as expected. Under the floorboard of the closet in the master bedroom. The husband came home in a hurry when she called him about the warrant, they both raised hell, they were decent honest citizens and if the police thought they could just walk in as if they were criminals, they'd get a lawyer and teach us different—but when I told them what we expected to find, they calmed down in a hurry. They've only been renting the place a year."

Maddox laughed. "What does it look like? Is there anything left to identify?"

"Negative. Mostly bones. This is really the damndest, Maddox. Well, we'll send it in and see what the doctors make of it."

Maddox, Feinman and Rodriguez sat there waiting for the other calls, but nothing had come through when a messenger dropped off a report. Maddox glanced at it idly; it was the autopsy report on that jumper, Robert Farrell. A minute later he sat up and said loudly, "What the bloody hell is this?"

"What?" asked Rodriguez, startled.

"This jumper—damn it, he'd just been seeing a head doctor! But he wasn't a suicide, for God's sake. The hyoid bone's broken—somebody strangled him. I'll be damned." And then the phone rang again and it was the sergeant in Corinth, New York. He sounded tentative, as if he didn't quite believe what he was saying, and that was understandable. They had gone to that address, the house Hinman had lived in until ten years ago, and looked, and they had found three bodies. At least, said the sergeant, mostly skeletons. There was a deep foundation, and one of the bodies had been on top of the other two.

"Three!" said Feinman, looking shaken.

"Well, he lived there for six years, after all," said Rodriguez. "My God, I hope all these householders can be persuaded to shut up, from letting it out to the press—if he knows we're on his trail he'll never show up anywhere—"

Maddox was laughing. "And you know, we haven't even got a snapshot of him—just a vague general description. The fat little shoe clerk. About five-five, and bald, and wears glasses. My God, when you think of it—"

The calls came in from Covina and Monterey Park after lunch. In Monterey Park, at the address where Hinman had lived when he first came to California ten years ago, they had found two bodies, partly mummified and partly skeletal, in the indicated place. In Covina, where he had moved eight years ago, and stayed until he moved to Pasadena, they had found two more.

Feinman said, "Ten! Ten altogether! I'm still not believing this— And where the hell has he gone? And why?"

They now had the temporary plate number in NCIC's computers, and a want out on him nationwide. Somebody was bound to spot that new Chevy sometime.

"Well, as I told your lieutenant," said Dr. Werner, "I was astonished to hear that Robert Farrell had committed suicide. He wasn't a suicidal subject. I had had him under treatment for several months and should know." He was a dapper round little man with a bald head and a big nose. "And in any case, I very strongly doubt that he would have jumped off a roof. He had a great fear of heights."

"Why were you treating him?" asked Maddox. "What do you know about him?"

"Practically everything there was to know. I suppose there's no harm in telling you now the man's dead. He was in treatment with me because he was deeply motivated to break out of a homosexual pattern. He had come under the influence of an unfortunately much stronger personality when he was just moving into adolescence, at the age of thirteen. The other male was four years older. He had become the only influence, in point of fact, ever since then—for some ten years. Robert was both repelled and attracted—on the one hand, the other man directed all his thought processes, gave him affection, money, support —and on the other hand, Robert resented his dependence on the other, and longed to be free of him."

"He was a fag, and he wanted out."

"He had tried to break his relationship with the other several times. But each time some crisis of monetary need or emotional distress had driven him back to the stronger character."

"The guy was supporting him," said Maddox, "and he didn't like to work at a regular job."

"Unfortunately Robert was weak in the basic skills of language. It was difficult for him to perform at a normal standard even on fairly simple tasks."

"He was graduated from school barely literate and couldn't hold a job," translated Maddox. Werner looked at him disapprovingly. "Where'd he get the money to come to you?"

Werner coughed. "I understand that an aunt somewhere in the east left him a legacy. He felt that perhaps, where he could not trust his own mental strength to keep him away from the destructive influence, with my active support he could succeed. It is a well-known axiom of psychiatric practice that it is necessary to transfer the patient's trust and affection to the physician, in order to effect any successful treatment. He—"

"Yes," said Maddox, who was tired of him. "Who's the guy? Do you know his name?"

"His name is Andrew Fanning. Though when Robert's dead I really don't see why you would be interested."

"You're not a detective, Doctor," said Maddox.

This time, when the night watch got a call to Curson Street, it was something different. It was Stacey's night off, and Brougham and Donaldson both went out on it.

The squad car man waiting for them as Jowett. "The poor woman was scared to death," he said. "She was still shaking when I got here, and I had to turn the flash on my badge before she let me in."

"What happened?"

"I don't know if you'd call it a burglary or a heist," said Jowett doubtfully. "She was sitting in her living room reading—she's a widow, lives here alone—when some punk broke in a bedroom window and held her up with a knife. He got away with all the money she had in her handbag, about twenty dollars."

Mrs. Frances Lamb was still shaking and scared. She was a little thin woman with a halo of white hair. "There are good locks," she said, repeating it like a litany. "There are good locks with dead bolts—my husband always said that was the important thing. Dead bolts. I'll never feel safe in this house again! He came right in—I heard the window break, and I thought, mercy, what's that?—and there he *was* and he had a knife in his hand—"

"Can you give us a description of him, what his face was like, Mrs. Lamb?" asked Brougham.

"Oh, no—that was what frightened me so! He looked like—like a man from Mars! He had something right over his face, his head, just a hole for his mouth and holes for eyes, it was a kind of tan, it squashed his face into just a blob—he looked like a monster, he was so big—"

"Nylon stocking," said Brougham tersely to Donaldson, who just nodded. "Did he touch anything in here, ma'am?"

"What do you mean? No, I don't think so—he asked for money and I took it out of my bag and gave it to him—all the bills—and he opened the front door and ran out, up the street, I guess. But there are good locks. Good locks and dead bolts."

So they would dust the door and see if they raised any prints. Outside, Brougham asked, "Think it's the mugger on this?"

"It sounds like him. Big and strong. But why the hell is he operating just on this couple of blocks? Does he live along here?"

"Unlikely," said Brougham.

Johnny McCrea called in a Code Seven at eight-thirty. He left the squad in a yellow zone right outside The Blue Note, and had his sandwich and coffee while he listened to the music. The old boys were really swinging up a storm tonight, he thought.

They had finished "I'll Get By" and were taking their usual midevening break when he should have been getting back to the squad. It happened just as he stood up. The door to the kitchen, facing the end of the bar on the left side, burst open and two men came in, in a hurry, and they both had guns out. They stopped short at the end of the bar and one of them said in a loud voice, "This is a stickup—" But there was the low buzz of conversation filling the room and the only people who heard that, noticed them, were the people at the front tables, the bartender and the four men in the combo.

It all happened in about four seconds. The men with the guns had their backs to the little platform, to their left and rear—they hadn't noticed it. Old Claude Delarue deliberately laid down the sax, took four steps to the edge of the platform and launched himself at the nearest heister's back, two feet away. The gunman went flat on his face, the gun going off and two bullets shattering the big mirror behind the bar, and the other man whirled half around and fired five shots. Delarue was on his knees on top of the first man, and he went down in slow motion, and sprawled on his back on the floor in front of the platform. The bartender brought a full bottle of Bourbon down on the second man's head and he went down. McCrea had his gun out by then and pushed people away, getting up there in a hurry. A few women had screamed at the shots.

Both the men were unconscious, and McCrea groped for his set of handcuffs, snapped them on in a hurry—it wasn't the kind of thing the training manual told you about—he thrust his gun at the bartender to hold the other if he came to, and he flung himself down on his knees beside Delarue. The little black piano player was there, closest, the other two behind.

"Cloudy—Cloudy—"

There was a spreading red stain on Delarue's white shirt. He opened vague eyes and saw Robson looking down at him. He gave Robson a faint grin. "Fella put in a request—for 'St. Louis Blues'—do it after the break—and, Artie, you make that keyboard talk pretty, hah?" He turned his head to one side like a tired child and died, and Robson began to cry, the tears running down his thin black cheeks, and suddenly McCrea felt like crying himself.

CHAPTER 10

Andrew Fanning showed up in records, just on one count a couple of years back. He had overestimated the age of a high school boy he was attempting to seduce, and so when the boy brought the cops in they could charge him with enticement. He got six months, suspended, which was about par for the course. His address at the time was in Beverly Hills.

Maddox and Rodriguez went out there on Saturday, to see if he was home. It was an expensive-looking apartment building on one of the newer streets, and Maddox said, "I wonder where the money comes from."

"He's too young to have made a bundle pimping—possibly he deals in the silly powder," said Rodriguez.

"The autopsy said Farrell wasn't a user."

They found the right apartment, and Rodriguez pushed the bell. They waited awhile before the door opened. "Andrew Fanning?"

"That's me." He recognized them instantly for what they were, and looked a little wary. He was tall and dark and just missed being handsome by near-set eyes and a crooked nose.

"About Robert Farrell," said Maddox, putting the badge away.

Fanning said, "Oh, yeah, poor old Bob, I never thought he'd do a thing like that, kill himself. He'd threatened to do it a couple times, but I never took it seriously."

"He did?" said Maddox. "Let's go in, shall we?" Fanning stepped back and they went into a living room anonymous with furniture supplied by the management. Ungraciously, Fanning said, "Sit down." He added, "I suppose you're just clearing up all the red tape, after what happened."

"That's about it," said Rodriguez. "Did you know Farrell was seeing a psychiatrist?"

Fanning was surprised. "No, I didn't. Was he?"

"That's strange, Mr. Fanning," said Maddox. "The psychiatrist told us that on several occasions Farrell had found you waiting for him when he left the office, that you were very angry with him about seeing the doctor."

Caught off guard, Fanning said weakly, "Oh, that doctor—well, I didn't think he was very good, that's all."

"Farrell had told him that you had threatened to beat him up if he tried to leave you."

"That's a lie, Bob was the best friend I had, damn it—"

"Yes, that was why, wasn't it?"

"You got it all wrong, I never—"

Maddox said, "And now try for the gold ring, Mr. Fanning. How did you know Farrell was dead?"

Fanning said, "Why, naturally—" He stopped. "Why, we had a date set up for the next night, when he didn't show up I went to his pad, and the manager told me—what had happened."

"That's a plausible effort," said Rodriguez, "but no, you didn't. The apartment Farrell lived in hasn't got a manager on the premises. He lived alone, and he hadn't any relatives here to notify. His parents live in Florida, and they'd thrown him out years ago, weren't interested in what happened to him. He was a loner, so the doctor says, and had hardly any acquaintances except for you. We notified the parents by wire, and we didn't talk to anybody at the apartment. There hasn't been anything about it in the news."

"How did you know, Mr. Fanning?" asked Maddox.

"I—" Fanning looked from one to the other of them.

"And you got one other thing wrong too," said Maddox. "He didn't commit suicide. He was murdered. Somebody strangled him, and we think it was you."

Fanning let his breath out in a little hiss and said, "How in hell did you know he was strangled, for God's sake? I thought he'd be a bloody pulp, twelve stories down—"

"The doctors have ways of telling," said Maddox. "You were waiting in the hall for him when he came out of the doctor's office, weren't you? You had another argument with him, trying to get him to stop seeing the psychiatrist. And you lost your temper and killed him. It's an easy way to kill anybody."

"I never meant to kill him, for Christ's sake. I couldn't believe he was dead—I'd just taken hold of him to shake some sense into him— damn it, I didn't—"

"And when you found he was dead," said Rodriguez, "you had the bright idea of taking him up to the roof, only one flight up, and throwing him off. Come on, we'll take you up to jail now."

Fanning said coldly, "You won't keep me there. My mother's got enough money to buy a battery of lawyers, and I'm her baby boy. You can't make out I meant to kill him, it was an accident, just a damn accident!"

"Listen," Dan Cass was saying to D'Arcy and Nolan, at the jail, "listen, it was an accident—they was both accidents, the people we killed out here! Jesus, the time we been havin', even a jail don't look too bad," and he looked around the little interrogation room almost gratefully. He was just a big dumb punk, and his brother Arnie was another one. "This is a damned awful place, we never rightly knew how awful it'd be till we got here—"

"How did you get here?" asked D'Arcy.

Arnie said despondently, "A right nice fella picked us up after the truck died on us, he was heading for California, he'd just got out of jail in some place named Duluth. But he said California was his home base. He was real nice, when he found out we was on the run from the sheriff he said best place to hide was a big town, and us never havin' been to a city we'd like it fine. Jesus, I don't know how anybody lives here without goin' crazy, honest, all the noise and people and colored signs whizzin' and goin' on and off—and we din't know how to get out! He got arrested just after he brought us here, he coulda showed us the ropes, but—"

"The cops wanted him for something he'd did back east," said Dan. "He said his name was Ray Green or something like that. But the cops din't arrest us and we still had his car, the cops din't know about that because we was on the sidewalk when they arrested him."

"Where was this?" asked D'Arcy.

They looked confused. "Jesus, I dunno," said Dan. "Some place, Anna or something."

"Santa Ana?" asked Nolan.

"I guess so. And we wanted to get out, and we couldn't find no way at'all! It was awful, we drove all over but there wasn't no end to the place, we never could get outta town, it just went on and on—and we ain't used to them funny traffic lights, and a lotta times cops yelled at us, we'd done somethin' wrong—and we got nervous the sheriff had found out where we'd headed and told the cops here—"

"And we din't have no money," Arnie took up the tale, "we hadda get some money to eat, and Jesus, what they charge just to eat, it's awful—but them places we stuck up din't have much money, we couldn't make it out—only place we got much was that liquor store, so we figured to find another one—"

Dan said with dogged logic, "I says it don't make sense there's no

way outta the damn town, it's got to come to an end sometime, if we go
by the sun and keep drivin' east we got to get out of it sometime. We
were goin' to hold up this other liquor store and maybe get enough
money to last awhile—"

"Then what were you doing in that bar?" asked Nolan.

Arnie said plaintively, "Jesus, we din't know it was that bar, we
thought that was the back door to that liquor store next door to it! But
we get in, there's this kitchen place with nobody there, so we walk
through this other door and Jesus, there's all those goddamn people—"

D'Arcy called Santa Ana. About three weeks ago a couple of Traffic
men there had spotted a wanted man walking down Main Street, and
picked him up. A flyer had gone out on him from Minnesota because
he had an ex-wife in Santa Ana. He was Ray Greenspan, a three-time
loser at bank robbery, and he'd gone over the wall from a federal
prison back there, so they'd bundled him up and sent him back to the
waiting arms. He hadn't had any car keys on him, and said he'd just
gotten to town on the bus. In fact, the car the Casses had been driving,
discovered in the parking lot behind the bar and grudgingly acknowledged, had been stolen from a doctor in Duluth.

D'Arcy looked at the Casses and thought about fate. There was
never any way to unravel it, or understand it—the innocent people
killed in Montana, the innocent people killed here.

"Where'd you get the guns?" he asked.

Dan said querulously, "That's another damn thing. This Ray, he
took us a place to get the guns, a place they call a pawnbroker—we got
these goddamned pieces, but we ain't never had much to do with hand-
guns, and they ain't like a decent shotgun—" He looked at them indig-
nantly, a hardly used man. "The damn things go off if you look
crooked at 'em!" he said.

The wants had been out on Hinman for three days, and the forces in
New Jersey and New York had a good many men on the hunt because
that would be the likeliest place he was holed up, if they could go by
the transferred bank accounts. The state police were covering a lot of
territory, looking. Everybody was hampered by the fact that they didn't
have a picture of him. Maddox had hauled in the two clerks from the
store in Long Beach, who had worked with him most recently, for a
session with the Identikit, but they had proved to be broken reeds.
Evidently they'd taken the manager so much for granted that they'd
never looked at him closely. "He's just ordinary," said one of them help-
lessly. "Just sort of medium, all ways. Why the hell are the cops so
interested in him?"

At least nothing had gotten into the media about it. The artist produced a sketch but both clerks said it wasn't much like him.

In the end, it was an anticlimax, how they dropped on the fat little shoe clerk. Somebody left an old clunker of a Ford stalled in one of the aisles of the parking lot behind the Century-Plaza Hotel, and a squad car from Central was sent up to check the registration and arrange for it to be towed in. As the uniformed man was doing that he happened to notice a car in the slot behind it, and the temporary plate number rang a bell in his head, so he consulted the list of A.P.B.'s posted on his dashboard, and there it was. Hinman's new Chevy.

Four detectives from Central went out there in a hurry and began to ask questions, but they met with blank stares until one of them with some common sense had a look at the register. He had signed in under his own name.

They all looked at him there in the detective office of the Hollywood station. The black sergeant from Pasadena was there, men from Monterey Park and Covina, and from Central, because they had all been so interested in him, in this far-out thing. But there wasn't anything monstrous or fearful about him. He was just a fat little man with a bald head and glasses, a rather benign expression on his round face, and he looked like a very ordinary and respectable citizen. He was wearing an expensive new navy-blue suit, a white shirt and navy tie.

He hadn't said much to the arresting officers; now he looked at all the detectives around him where he sat in the straight chair beside Maddox's desk, and said, "Those other police officers said you want me for murder. How did you find out about it?" He sounded merely surprised and interested.

Maddox said, "We identified Rose Parfitt, Hinman." Rose Parfitt was the only one they could establish identity on, a name and an approximate date with a link to him; and he'd only be charged with that homicide. Unless he gave them names on the rest, nobody would ever know who they'd been.

He sighed sharply. "That's queer," he said. "I never thought anyone would ever find out. But you did—and it's queer that it should be—through that one—you did. I nearly let her go—I was really put out at that woman. I'd been working on her for a little while, and she was a good prospect—that ten thousand dollars—and then I found out she had a sister here. But I thought it over carefully, and came to the conclusion that it would be safe enough. She was feeling a little embarrassed to tell the sister about me, she said, only a year after losing her husband, and it would be time enough when the sister and her husband got back from that trip. So I hurried matters along and persuaded her and did it at once, and there was no trouble, I wasn't linked with her in any obvious way."

"How did you get her to give you her money?" asked Feinman.

"Why, of course she agreed to put all our money together, when we were married."

"You married her?" asked Maddox.

"Why, I married all of them," he said simply. "They were all respectable women." He didn't seem to mind talking about it; perhaps now that it was all out in the open, it was a relief to talk about it, even to feel some pride in an extraordinary accomplishment. He didn't express any remorse, any consciousness of guilt. He sat there quietly, a very ordinary-looking man, and he said with a little sigh, "There are so many of them, you know. The respectable lonely women. Most of them are widows, or divorcées. The kind of women who are working at dull little jobs, don't know many people—lonely. Women in their forties and fifties. They've been married before, and they've lost any romantic ideals about marriage—what they appreciate is a man of reliability, the security and companionship. And I look so very respectable, you know. I lost my hair quite young, I've always looked older than I am. A man in a good secure job, with a little money saved—women like that, they know they've got nothing to offer of looks or youth, they're grateful for attention, and it was the companionship angle that attracted them. And the security. Sex," said Hinman primly, "had nothing to do with it. Lonely women, without any relatives, just casual acquaintances—living in cheap rented places—who was to notice when they moved, didn't show up again? In big cities, there are more of them than you'd think. A very good place to find them" —and his tone was nearly that of a lecturer—"is libraries, because they aren't shy of talking to a stranger at a library, it's such an innocent place. Queerly enough, about the next best place is spiritualist meetings. When you find a middle-aged woman alone at a spiritualist meeting, it's practically a guarantee that she hasn't any family or close friends. Churches, sometimes. Most regular churchgoers have friends in the congregation, but once in a while you run across one at a big city church who goes just to pass the time. In fact, I met a very good prospect that way once, she was worth nearly twenty thousand."

They were all regarding him somewhat aghast at his ready talk, his matter-of-fact attitude. "Why?" asked Ellis bluntly. "Just for the money?"

"Why, of course," he said blandly. "The first time, that was what really gave me the idea and made me realize how easy it was. That was my first wife. You see, I don't really enjoy being married, living with anyone—I'm a quiet man, I like to read, and I have my own little routine ways—I'd been married to Gertrude for a year, she was a very strong-minded woman, and I found her annoying in several ways. She always had the radio on," he said reminiscently. "And when I was asked to transfer to the store in Warrensburg, I saw how easy it would be. We had friends in Glassboro, people who knew us, but not close friends. Nobody would think it odd if we lost touch after moving."

"That's the one in Glassboro?" asked Maddox.

"Yes, Gertrude. She had just had that legacy from her aunt, and of course we had put it in our joint account. When I transferred the account to Warrensburg I simply put it under my name only. I got rid of Gertrude the night before we were supposed to move."

"How?" asked Rodriguez. "How did you kill them?"

He didn't seem disconcerted by the one word. "Oh, the simplest way. A garrote from behind. The method perfected by the Thuggees in India, you know. It's quick, quiet and easy. It doesn't take much strength, actually, and they were dead within thirty seconds. No one in Warrensburg knew I had been married, and of course no one ever knew about the other wives at all—well, until the last one. Well, they were wives such a short time," he reflected, looking into the past. "Lester's is open on Sundays, they began the policy during the Depression, and I was always able to arrange that I was off on a weekday. There, you see, I was in easy distance of the Albany-Schenectady-Troy area, a large city area with a large population. Really there were more suitable prospects available than I could have handled. It was only when I found a really good prospect—a widow with insurance, the husband's savings— All of those, back there, were delighted at the prospect of acquiring a comfortable humdrum husband and moving to a smaller town." He smiled tenderly. "I would arrange the marriage for a Sunday, in the city, and of course I always had them get cashier's checks to be deposited in our joint account, so there was no way to trace the money to me. We would arrive at the house after dark—they thought it was a house my first wife and I had owned together. None of the neighbors ever knew they had been there. As soon as we were safely inside, I'd do the job."

Maddox asked, "Why did you quit the job with Lester's, Hinman? Change all the bank accounts?"

He looked tired suddenly; his round face sagged. "I'm fifty-seven years old. It suddenly came to me, what have I ever had out of life? I hadn't been feeling too well lately. All my life, the dull job—and I had accumulated quite a little money. It all added up, you know."

Feinman said, "My God," under his breath.

"Unfortunately most of it had been deposited in banks, to look natural, and I had to pay taxes on it. But I had managed to get some of it out, over a period of time, and safely put away." That, they knew: he'd had over twenty thousand dollars on him when he was picked up. "I thought, I've never really had a vacation—enjoyed myself just relaxing. Working so hard all my life. I could afford to retire early. I thought it might be pleasant to go back east again—and I transferred those accounts—but then I thought, well, I like the climate here. I hadn't decided what to do. And I'd never stayed at a really nice expensive hotel before—I'd been there for nearly three weeks, and it was very pleasant. Very pleasant indeed."

"Why," asked Feinman, "did you keep the one in Long Beach alive so long—introduce her to the landlord?"

"Oh, Muriel. She was a really excellent plain cook—really quite a nice woman. But in the end I got so very tired of her passion for TV. I really prefer," said Hinman, "to live alone."

Ellis said, "You've married ten women—over thirty years—and murdered them—and you prefer—?"

Hinman looked up at him, astonished. "Ten? Oh, my goodness, there were many more than that—a great many more! When I ran out of space under the house there was always the backyard—I always took care to choose a place not overlooked by neighbors. Do you mean to say you've only found ten?"

That rendered them speechless; they didn't ask him any more questions then.

That night Mr. John Danner had been working late on the books, in his little furniture store on Vermont Avenue, and didn't get home until about nine-thirty. As he got out of his car in the driveway, a hulking figure sprang out of the darkness and fell on him. Mr. Danner was fifty-four, only five-seven and a scant hundred and forty pounds, but during his spell in the service he had mastered the art of jujitsu.

When Brougham and Stacey got up to Curson Street, he said to them, "I'm afraid I've broken his arm."

Sitting in the back of the squad car was a great big burly kid—over six feet and big-boned, but by his face he couldn't be over sixteen. "I didn't realize it was the Sawyer boy," said Danner. "Jack Sawyer. Why, he lives right across the street, his parents are nice people. Why he should do a thing like this—he always seemed a good enough kid. I'd put him out cold and called the police before I took a look at him, or I'd just have spoken to his father."

The kid was whimpering and nursing his arm. He looked at them resentfully, bitterly. "He like to've killed me! I just hadda get some money—you got to have money, for lots o' things at school, takin' girls out—and Dad cut off my whole damn allowance till I start gettin' better grades and it wasn't fair no ways—"

"We're very glad you called us, Mr. Danner," said Stacey. They both looked at the kid, and they thought about Esther Cook, and they felt very tired.

Sue was, for some reason, having a white night. She had drifted off for about an hour, and now she was wide awake, with no prospect of getting back to sleep. Maddox was slumbering peacefully. She went down to the bathroom for a drink of water, and Tama came to the door of Margaret's room enquiringly. "It's all right," Sue whispered, stroking his great heavy head. "You go back to sleep." She sat in the chair by the window in the bedroom, smoking an occasional cigarette. She was wide awake as an owl.

It grew gradually colder, and she snuggled back into bed. Half an hour before the alarm would go off, she prodded Maddox awake. "Listen, Ivor—are you really awake?—I've been thinking."

He yawned and half sat up. "What are you doing awake at this hour? About what?"

"Come on, sit up and have a cigarette—are you really awake now?" He was a very good-tempered husband, and didn't complain much. When he was provided with a cigarette and the bedside lamp was on, she said, "I've been thinking about the real mother. Of the Mainwaring son. You know, women are funny creatures."

"Now you tell me."

"Avis said, some little slut. But, you know, Mainwaring being the kind he was, it wouldn't have been. Are you following me? He'd have been—particular—about a woman he hired to bear a child for him. Bloodlines and so on."

Maddox, further awake, said, "Well, I follow that. What about it?"

"Where did he find her? Who was she? Because a woman like that, not just a tramp—of course she might have been just greedy for money —but there aren't many women who'd agree to do such a thing. And I just wonder about her."

"Connected with the murder?"

"No—maybe—I don't know. I don't expect so, not really. But if she's —around somewhere, I just wonder—if she ever wondered—about the baby—and found out anything. Damn," said Sue, "it's probably just vulgar curiosity. But there might be something in it."

Maddox pulled her closer against his shoulder. "When a legal adoption goes through, the names of the adoptive parents are put on a new birth certificate as the real parents, and the original birth certificate is locked up in Vital Statistics in Sacramento."

"Yes, and we can get a court order to get a copy of it if we ask. We're privileged."

"Do you want to do that?"

"Yes, I think I do. There's probably nothing in it at all, and the woman was just some honest not very sensitive girl who wanted the money and never thought about the baby at all, ever since. But if she wasn't—"

"Well?"

"I don't know."

"In fact, it's just a feeling. Well, I can ask for the court order. You know the red tape. It may take a while."

"Yes, I know." And then the alarm went off and they both jumped.

Maddox had nearly forgotten about that in the spate of daily work coming along. The press had already forgotten Roy Kelsey when the Hinman thing broke on a fascinated nation. Several police forces were still hunting for bodies, and none of the bodies was, probably, going to get identified; Hinman himself admitted that he didn't remember names. The wives had been so fleeting, had become bodies so soon. The only exception, besides Rose Parfitt, was the first wife, Gertrude. The oldest body, back in Glassboro. Hinman was up for indictment next week. Legally speaking, the only evidence they had was on Parfitt, and he'd be charged with Murder One on that, probably get life. By all the reports, Hinman was getting a great kick out of all the publicity.

And of course other things had come along. They now had a messy rape-homicide which was all up in the air. There was the usual parade of heisters around, and always the burglaries. There had been a daylight heist at a big post office branch, and the postal inspectors were coming and going out of the station; one of them was a nice fellow, but the other one inclined to surliness. It was the consensus of opinion that he had an ulcer. This morning another homicide had gone down, and it looked like a rather anonymous thing, housewife surprised by a burglar, but you never knew—remembering May Reuther, Maddox wanted to know more about the housewife.

He came back to the station late that Wednesday feeling stale and tired. It was raining again and looked as if it was going to go on raining for a while. Nolan was the only one still in, finishing a report. Maddox had only come back to see if that autopsy report had showed up; it hadn't, and he swore. But there was something else on his desk, a long business-size manila envelope with the official state seal. Bureau of Vital Statistics.

Nolan was putting on his coat. "D'Arcy took off early. He had a date."

"Good," said Maddox. "So he's found a new girl." He slit the envelope.

"Er—" said Nolan. "I wanted to ask somebody—the lieutenant warned me that he's very touchy about his first name, but I never heard what it is."

"If you promise to forget it, I'll tell you. It's Drogo."

"My God," said Nolan. "I've already forgotten it." He went out.

And Maddox took out the slip of paper inside the envelope and looked at it, without much interest. He'd only been obliging Sue on this.

It was the original birth certificate. And he read it, and said blankly to himself, "But if it's the same one—what the hell could it say?"

Baby boy, eight pounds, three ounces. Caucasian. A date. And, illegitimate. Name of father, Charles Mainwaring. Name of mother, Kathleen French.

"What the hell?" said Maddox.

When she opened the door to them, it was the same one. The address had been in the phone book. She looked at Maddox and said, "Oh, you came to the office—that day." She looked at the badge.

"That's right, Mrs. French." He put the badge away, introduced Sue. "We just want to talk to you a few minutes, if you don't mind." She brought them in, to a typical pleasant middle-class apartment living room, and they sat together on the couch, facing her in an opposite chair.

"What is it you want to ask?" she said dully. She was looking ill, and her thin face was haggard.

"I want to show you something." And he handed her the birth certificate.

She looked at it without showing any expression. Then she raised her eyes and looked past them at the opposite wall for a long, rapt moment. She looked more than her probable age, a woman once ordinarily pretty; she had kept a good figure, but the tinted brown hair harshened her complexion. She asked, "Are you going to arrest his wife for the murder? Or his son?"

"I don't think we're going to arrest anybody," said Maddox. "There's not enough evidence. We may have suspected this and that, but there's not enough evidence for a legal charge."

"I see," she said. "Why did you go looking—for this?"

"Intuition," said Sue.

She read it again, and suddenly her hand clenched on it so tightly the knuckles turned white. She said, "It's very queer that you came here to-night. Because I was coming to see you tomorrow. Because I haven't paid enough—I haven't done enough. Maybe I never will. I was going to tell you a lie, about why I did it. That I was having an affair with him, and was jealous. But since you've seen this—only I wouldn't want the truth getting out—everybody knowing."

"Police keep secrets, Mrs. French, quite a lot of them. But if—"

"It's only important to me, I suppose. Officially—"

And then she was silent so long that Sue asked, "Where did you first meet him?"

"I never knew him really," said Kathleen French. "I only saw him twice—then. I'd just gotten the divorce from Rex. I never wanted anything to do with a man again. I really got burned with Rex French. He cured me of marriage. Period. But I was broke, he'd skipped with all our savings. And I saw this ad, in the *Times*. A box number. I laughed at it at first because it was so funny—what they call a surrogate mother —have a baby for somebody. And then I looked at it again, it said ten thousand dollars and all expenses—and I thought, why not? Why not? I was all alone, nobody to care what I did. I think I answered it out of curiosity, a little, too. It asked for family history, references."

"I said he'd do that," said Sue.

"I wonder how many answers he got," said Maddox.

"I wouldn't know. I shouldn't think many. He wrote and asked me to meet him. It was an empty office in a professional building on Wilshire. He was all business. He'd asked me to bring all the family papers I had, he wanted to know all about my family, nationalities and so on. It's quite a nice family, you know, two ministers back a way, and he seemed pleased that it was all English and Welsh on both sides."

Maddox laughed shortly.

"He said, ten thousand dollars, and an extra five thousand if it was a boy. And I'd be paid five hundred a month till the baby came and all the medical expenses. He asked if I was willing to do it. His wife couldn't have children, he said, and they wanted a family. That was a lot of money then. And as I say, I hadn't anybody to care or notice what I did. I thought about the money—and I said I'd do it.

"He took me to a doctor's office, an old shabby place but the doctor was nice. He did it—you know—artificially. And the money was fine, a cashier's check every month, and I felt fine the whole time. For the last two weeks I was in a private maternity clinic in Santa Monica, a really first-class place, they were wonderful to me. It probably cost him a lot. I never saw the baby. I knew it was a boy because I got the extra five thousand." She smiled at Sue. "You're probably thinking I'm pretty cold-blooded, and you're right—I was. But I was still hurting from Rex, I wanted to crawl into a hole and forget the world. I didn't think about the baby very often. Not at all, really. It wasn't very real to me, that time. And then about fourteen years ago I saw Mainwaring's picture in the *Times*—it was some realtors' association dinner—and of course I recognized him. I'd never known his name, you see. And two years after that something very queer happened. I wasn't too happy with the job I was in, and I answered an ad in the classified, for a qualified personnel assistant. It would be a step up for me, and more money. I had a good résumé, and they hired me. And I never knew it was his company—I'd thought he was a realtor. When I found out, I was scared—I wanted that job, and if he recognized me—but he'd hardly looked at me, back then, and it had been sixteen years ago. But I thought he might remember my hair, so I had it tinted. But he never looked twice at me. I didn't see him often, he didn't come down to Accounting much.

"I hadn't thought about the baby in years. And then—then he came into the office. Last year, in August. He was born in August, I'd nearly forgotten that. And something very funny happened to me. He looked so much like—his father—but he had hair just like mine, the same color. And—the first time—Mr. Schultz called him down for something, and said he was stupid, I was furious—I was just furious. He didn't look stupid to me, he looked—clever.

"And it got to be an obsession. I'd make excuses to go past his desk, just to see him. And every time I saw him—I'd think, if it weren't for me you wouldn't be alive. It was queer, you just can't imagine how queer it was, to look at him and know—he'd been part of my body. It was as if—I couldn't see him enough. Just to be looking at him. But that night—that night—" she clenched her hands on the birth certificate tightly.

"What happened that night?" asked Sue quietly.

"He was in the elevator with me when we left the building. Neither of us said anything, but he looked so worried and troubled, I wondered why. Somehow I just couldn't bear him to be worried—unhappy. I wanted to ask him what was wrong, try to help him. He drove out of the lot just ahead of me, and we both went down Sunset—" This apartment was in West Hollywood. "And I should have turned on Havenhurst but I wondered where he was going, to a date with a girl or what.

I followed him, and a few blocks on he turned into the lot of a restaurant. I felt like a fool, I didn't know why I was there, there was no way I could help him, but I thought— Well, I parked and went in. He was outside, waiting for somebody. He didn't see me. The waiter put me in a booth right at the back—and when he came, he was with another man, they sat in the next booth, right behind me."

She drew a long breath. "And so I heard—all of it. He was doing all the talking, not loud but I could hear. Those high-backed booths, they look like solid wood and you feel private, but—I heard it all, he was pouring it all out to his friend. I could guess—from some things he said—how it had been all his life. Oh, every advantage, plenty of money—*he* said that, all those years ago—but they never gave him any of what's important, love and kindness and real caring. And I heard all about—the trouble between him and his father—and about that great artist who thinks he could be a great painter too, and that school he wanted to go to—and how he was caught, with no way out. No way out, he said. He said, by this time next week I'll be out in the cold, and I don't know what the hell to do about it. How his father was going to make that new will and not leave him anything. And when they left, I sat there for a long, long time. I was doing all the thinking I should have done nearly twenty-four years ago. The waiter hinted that I should go, and I ordered a bottle of wine and sat there drinking it."

She'd been talking directly to Sue for some time, ignoring Maddox. "Can you understand what I was thinking? I saw exactly what I'd done —just how completely selfish and irresponsible I'd been. I'd sold him, for fifteen thousand dollars. It's against the law to sell human beings, isn't it? I'd sold him—the way a person might hand over a puppy or a kitten, without bothering to find out if it'd have a good home. Something I was responsible for, that could feel pain and be unhappy, and I hadn't given it a thought, I hadn't cared. I sat there for a long, long time. For twenty-three years. Thinking.

"And I thought about that stupid, stupid man. Couldn't he see what a much finer thing it might be to have a son who was a great artist, than one who could just run a business? And the whole thing was all my fault because I'd been stupid too—it was my fault but it was his too, and I thought if I didn't do something about it I wouldn't have an excuse to go on living.

"The restaurant was closing. I drove home. I'd bought a gun a couple of years ago when we had a rape in the building. I had to look up the address. And I didn't know but what there'd be a crowd of people there, his wife, a party. I thought I'd just ask to see him alone, and do   M37 it. I didn't care what happened to me afterward. You see, there was no way I could ever pay enough for what I'd done, make it up, if I spent the rest of my life trying. But if I killed him, before he could make that will, it would save the boy." She hadn't once spoken his name. "But there wasn't a party. He was alone in the house. And of course when he saw me he thought it was something to do with the office. I said it was about one of the employees, Mr. Hauser had sent me, and he took me back to his study. As soon as he sat down—I was beside the desk, and he wasn't looking at me—I just took out the gun and shot him. I made sure he was dead, and went away. But I've been thinking about it ever since, and it isn't enough—nothing's ever going to be enough—and I ought to pay for killing him, because that was wrong too. I was going to the police tomorrow." She looked at Maddox then. "Does it all have to come out—at a trial? I wouldn't want—him—to know. Even when I deserve to have him hate me and blame me—I wouldn't want him to know. Can't I just say—I was having an affair with his father and was jealous?"

"That's up to you, Mrs. French," said Maddox. "You can say that, and it could be just a hearing before a judge, and sentencing. But I think you'd better give me that gun now."

"It's in the drawer of the end table beside you. I wouldn't use it to shoot myself. That would be too easy," she said listlessly.

It was late when they got home, and they hadn't done much talking about it. There wasn't much to say. The rain hadn't let up much and it was supposed to go on raining the rest of the week. Margaret was sitting reading in the living room when they came in, with Tama at her feet.

"Goodness, you are late. Sue, you look awfully tired—you'd better go straight to bed, and I'll get you a glass of hot milk."

Sue dropped her coat over a chair. "I've just decided," she said broodingly, "that there's something rather frightening about having a baby. Not just having it, but all the awful responsibility."

"You're not running a temperature, are you?" Margaret got up, looking worried.

Maddox laughed and put an arm around each of them. "No, she's just having horrible examples shoved at her, on the job. The thankless dirty job. So am I. And it's another day tomorrow, and probably something new turning up to show us some more human nature in action. We'd all better get some sleep."

About the Author

Elizabeth Linington has written more than fifty novels. Among her previous novels featuring Ivor and Sue Maddox are *Consequence of Crime, No Villain Need Be,* and *Perchance of Death.*